BETRAYED The Eyes of the Tiger

BETRAYED, Volume 2

Kezel Romanoff

Published by Kezel Romanoff, 2023.

BETRAYED THE EYES OF THE TIGER

First edition. April 5, 2023.

Copyright © 2023 Kezel Romanoff.

ISBN: 978-1735927374

Written by Kezel Romanoff.

Dedicated to those whom their country have abandoned on foreign soil in order to cover the political mistakes made in times of, and, after war.

CHAPTER ONE

It was daybreak and overcast when everyone began to stir. Looking over at Arek, asleep behind the steering wheel and seeing the thick spruce forest out the window, gave me pause. It took a moment to remember. The tanks..., how they killed Tomas before we could escape; The deadly fight me, Arek, and Stefon had with Zarkhov, that produced two more people to care for in our effort to make it to the coast. Taking a deep breath, I shoved the car door open and stepped out into the cold morning air to relieve myself on the closest tree.

Hearing two other doors open, I pulled out a cigarette and lit it, figuring I'd give the women who joined us, a moment to step into the trees before turning around.

Finished with my smoke, I climbed back in as Arek slid in behind the wheel. Within minutes, the back door squeaked shut. Glancing over the seat, I tapped Arek's shoulder and nodded. He started the car and backed out of the woods to the gravel road. Trying not to hit my head on the dashboard every time we hit a pothole, I searched under the seat and in the glove box for papers, maps, anything that could tell us where we were.

Stefon, in the mean time, tried to make small talk with the new woman about her bloody companion and even offered to administer last rites should the time arise. Weeping, the woman whispered softly as she rocked her friend, "The time has already come, Father. Masha died while we were asleep."

Stefon struggled to perform the ritual while Arek swerved dodging potholes in the road. Finally putting his cross inside his shirt, he asked, "You seem familiar, may I ask your name?"

"I'm Katya..." the young woman wiped at her tears, "I worked with Masha in the clothing section."

I looked over at Arek. He nodded in acknowledgment to my unspoken question while staying focused on the road. Scanning

1

through the few papers I found, I sniped at him, "I thought she looked familiar."

"You know who I am because Masha told you," Katya insisted.

Tossing a few of the papers in my hands on the floor board, I asked, "Who you talking to?"

"You," she snapped.

Not wanting to acknowledge her, I kept pawing through the junk in the glove box. It was something to do even though I couldn't read Russian.

She bumped the back of my seat. "You got something to say?"

"No," I shrugged. "Not really."

A single sheet of colored paper with hand drawn lines that looked like roads on it caught my attention. "Ah, now we have something," I said as I held up the map. "Can anybody read Russian?"

The sound of the car's motor muffled their response. I looked over my shoulder at Katya. Turning away, she stared out the window. "I'm Evenki, not Russian."

I held the paper over the seat to her. "So you can read it, right?"

She cradled Masha's lifeless body with one arm and snatched the paper from my hand. "You're an ass."

Indifferent to her comment, I wrinkled my nose and turned forward waiting for her to say, 'we're right here'.

Arek pulled over and stopped. "If it helps, there's a river close by." He pointed toward a hill with a clearing on top. "There must be a town close by, too."

While Katya studied the map, Arek tapped me on the arm, motioning for me to follow him. Getting out and walking down the road, I half expected him to say something about her. Instead, he walked ahead of me in silence. As we rounded the next curve in the road, a wide river became visible in the distance. It flowed along the base of several low lying hills with a village spread between the base of their slopes. The skyline of the town impressed me. A mix of concrete high rises and two-story buildings with the forested hills on both sides.

My Polish comrade finally broke his silence. "There, at the edge of the trees..." he pointed towards the top of a hill down the road. "See the dome. There's a church there. We should be able to find shelter close by."

"What about being spotted?" I asked.

"No worry. The Soviets have destroyed most of the rural churches and sent the priests to prison." He tugged on my sleeve. "Let's go check it out."

My gut feeling was to go get the rifle from the car first.

Arek, however, stepped off the road and started picking his way through the brush. Shaking my head, I watched as he stepped off the road, *Yeah, that's what I like about you Arek, so damn secure in your decisions. I... Damn it, let's hope your right.*

Finding the church cemetery first, many of the stone markers leaned as if they had fallen from the sky. Carefully walking through the knee high grass, I half expected them to finish tipping over. At the bottom of the sloping graveyard, sat a large wooden building with an onion-shaped dome. Beyond it, a small clearing opened all the way down to the river. The church building itself, looked more like a fancy old barn with all its windows broken and doors torn from their hinges, than a place of worship.

On the stone steps leading up to the entrance, Arek spoke his opinion of what must have happened as we surveyed the integrity of the structure. "Most likely it was an old monastery that was poor and dying off when the local politburo needed to fill their quota for the work camps."

I peeked through the opening of a broken window. It had that musty odor of an abandoned house. "Looks fine to me," I said, turning to leave. "Let's go back and get the others so we can give Masha a decent burial."

Arek shuffled to the edge of the steps, then held his ground while staring towards the river. "Oh. So you did care about her."

"Don't be absurd. It was merely business between us."

"Ahh, you really are a gypsy," he snorted.

Angered by the insinuation, I made a fist wanting to thump him on the back of the head. Instead, biting my tongue, I quietly lit a cigarette. He brushed past me breaking the cigarette in my hand. Throwing it on the ground, I yelled at him, "Fuck you. We did—" Thoughts of Masha's antics flashed before my eyes making it too hard to finish my rant.

Getting back to the car just before dark, Arek jumped into the driver's seat and started the engine. I stood there, gazing through the window at Masha's lifeless body still in Katya's arms.

Arek mumbled, "Get in, Kezel," as he put the car in gear.

I slipped into the front seat and slammed the door. As the car lurched forward I hit the dashboard with the heel of my hand, howling, "That fuckin' bastard. I should have killed him in the woods when I had the chance. Then she'd still be alive."

Driving up the road, Arek pulled around behind the church in an effort to hide the car. With the flashlight I found in the glove box tucked under my arm, Arek and I carried Masha's body gingerly over the uneven stone floor, placing her on the fireplace hearth. Stefon continued preforming ritual prayers while he and Katya followed us with lit candles.

Placing his candle on the mantle, Katya put hers next to the body and started fussing with Masha's torn clothing. Stefon stood next to them and continued mumbling something in Polish while waving his hand around in circles.

I tapped Arek's arm. "Let's go get some firewood and check the car. Maybe there's something in it to dig her grave with."

He shook his head. "Kezel, there is nothing in this world—"

I spun around, shoving my palm in his face. "Don't!"

Giving him the evil-eye for a moment before taking a deep breath, I slowly exhaled, then walked outside afraid of what he was going to say...knowing I wasn't ready to hear it.

At the car, Arek fumbled through the trunk, while I pawed around under the seats. Reaching up to the seat springs under the driver's side I felt a cloth. It was wrapped around something heavy. Pulling the cloth out and laying it on the seat, I unwrapped the pistol and its holster. Grinning, I held up the handgun. "Hot damn! Arek, look what I just found."

He didn't look, instead he whispered loud enough for me to hear, "Praise God! Our prayers have been answered."

I slung the holster over my shoulder and walked over next to him. "What's better than...holy shit." My jaw dropped at the sight of the three boxes of canned food, a fourth box full of boots, and another with jewelry, watches, and cartons of cigarettes. A half-dozen bottles of vodka were dispersed amongst the boxes. There were even several packages of ammo for the rifle wedged in between the food boxes.

The illumination from the dim trunk light, reflected off one of the watches catching my attention. Picking it up, I read its inscription: *Tomas Hobbs, Saigon 1968-.*

"Fuckin' Zarkhov. That asshole made the damn urkis look like choir boys."

I strapped the watch around my wrist as Arek picked up a pillowcase from the spare tire well and peeked inside. His eyes nearly popped out. Hugging the cloth bag, he raised his face to the night sky, laughing, "Yes!"

It had to be something good to get that kind of reaction out of him. I waited a moment for him to show me. After his babbling 'yes' for the third time, I grabbed hold of the bag. "What's in it?"

Opening the bag, he held it out. "This is going to make buying food and petrol so much easier."

"Whew doggies! Look at all that. Let's take it inside and count it," I said, weighting the bag with my hands.

"No." Arek's face soured. "I know Stefon...and I trust him. But I can't say I know Katya that well. She might take the money and run in the middle of the night."

Seeing the uncertainty of his girl friend, reminded me of how Masha had played me in the beginning. I handed him the bag. "You're right. Let's get some firewood and go in."

Entering into the room with an arm load of wood and seeing only Stefon kneeling next to Masha, I dropped the wood on the hearth. "Where's Katya?"

Pointing towards another door, he stopped praying just long enough to mumble, "She found a pail and went towards the river."

Arek stepped through the door in time to hear his friend. Glancing at me with wide eyes, he tossed his load of wood on the floor. "I'll check on her."

Listening to Stefon's mumblings as I scraped a piece of wood making shavings to start a fire with, I finally had to ask, "What are you praying for? That her soul be rescued from hell?" Grabbing some twigs and breaking them into pieces, I tossed them onto the shavings. "Or that she comes back to life?"

He paused, crossed himself, then sat back on his haunches. "Are you trying to compare this life to hell?"

I grunted at my effort to break another handful of twigs, "What would you call it." Trying a second time and failing, I threw the unbroken handful on the pile and looked at him. "I mean, with what had just happened back there, in prison and all."

"My friend, you still have a lot to learn. Hell is forever, your time here is but a tick of the clock." He rose to his feet and moved closer as a small flame came to life in the pile of shavings. "There is nothing we can do for her physical body. I was praying for the intervention of her soul and for our well-being."

"I would then have to say your prayers have been answered." Struggling with breaking a large limb, I grunted, "We have a car...a rifle...and a few items to barter with."

Staring at the small flame, he held out his hands, fingering the smoke. "And how close to Poland will that get us?"

Tossing the limb into the flame, I stared at him in disbelief. "We're escaped prisoners. We killed a fuckin' federal guard. Stole his car..." I picked up another piece of wood, "and immediately you want to go back to where they threw your ass in jail." Gritting my teeth, I chucked the wood onto the growing flame. "We wouldn't make it to Moscow before getting executed."

"If you make that fire any bigger we'll be shot here," Arek said as he entered the room trailed by Katya carrying a pail of water. "There's a town across the river. If you make that fire any bigger, the flickering light will give us away."

Katya put her bucket down. "We don't need a fire to heat the water. Masha won't notice how cold it is." Tearing a small piece of cloth from Masha's shirt, she dipped it in the bucket. Gently, Katya began washing the bloody dirt from her friend's face. "At least we can give her a decent burial."

Grabbing a sprig of spruce from the wood pile, I held it out to Katya. "And how do you propose we do that? We don't have a shovel."

Arek walked over to her and placed his hands on her shoulders. Squeezing them, he whispered, "There's enough brick and stone from the tumbled down cemetery wall to build her a tomb."

"She was such a caring person." Katya's almond-shaped eyes filled with tears. "I will miss her."

Hearing the emotions in her comment, I jerked my thumb in Stefon's direction. "He thinks we should go back to Poland."

Before Arek could respond, Katya started wailing, "Masha, Masha, why didn't you run when I told you?"

The tall blond Pole nodded to me as he continued to rub Katya's shoulders.

My jaw dropped. "You two are fuckin' nuts!" I kicked a piece of wood across the room.

"Oh, Masha, I'm going to miss you. How will I ever—"

"Look!" I tried raising my voice over hers, "We're wanted prisoners in the West." Katya sobbing and wailing grew louder as she continued to wash the blood from Masha's hair.

I tried to carry my ranting on over her noise, "I say we go south, towards India."

"Through Tibet?" Arek raised an eyebrow. "Might be possible."

"Masha," Katya cried, "you would have looked better with red hair like you kept saying."

"With a car it should be so much easier," I offered between her anguished cries.

Stefon tossed more wood on the fire. "And how do you propose we set Poland free from India?"

"Masha, my love, you are free now. I am jealous that you can go home."

I snorted at Katya's comment. "We all want to go home."

Jumping to her feet, she slapped me with the bloody wet rag. "Shut up! Have you no feelings for her? She talked of you all the time."

Riled at the stinging of my cheek, I snapped back, "Our relationship was merely business."

"You bastard!" She took a swing at me again.

Bear hugging her, Alex lifted her off the ground. Crying, Katya fought to get free, then gave in to his effort to console her and settled down. Arek gave me that look, telling me I had just screwed up.

I hung my head offering, "I'm sorry, I didn't mean to sound cruel." After a moment of silence, I brushed the hair out of my eyes. "And, you're right. We have time to talk about directions later. We need to take care of Masha first." Looking over at Stefon, I motioned, "There has to be a spot somewhere in that yard, come help me make her a place of rest. Would you please?"

He balked. "We have no shovels. How do you plan to dig one?"

Having no desire to get into it with Katya again, I spun on my heels and walked towards the door. "With sticks and my hands, if need be. She deserves more than being dumped in the brush like we did Zarkhov."

* * *

We quietly laid Masha in her shallow grave by the light of the moon, then gently pushed the dirt over her. Solemnly, the four of us walked throughout the cemetery picking up stones and bricks, stacking them over Masha's grave until she was well protected. With the last stone, we stood around her in silence. Then Stefon, reaching down, picked up a handful of dirt. He weighed it in his hand. Holding the handful out, he spoke in Latin as he sprinkled it over her grave.

When the last of the dirt left his hand, he started to walk away. But before he got two steps away, I remembered what was in the car. "Wait! We're not finished yet. Everyone stay here, I'll be right back."

Snatching a bottle of the vodka from the car's trunk, I held it close as I rushed back to the grave. Twisting the cap off, I looked at the others as I held the opened bottle above the pile of stones. "To my comrade...partner...lover, until we meet again." I poured a small amount on her grave...then took a swig myself.

Gasping for breath, I held out the bottle to Katya.

Taking it, she poured a little over the pile of stones. "My love, until we meet again." She took a hefty swig and passed the bottle to Arek. Repeating the ritual, he offered, "Till we meet again, my friend." Handing it off to Stefon, the priest took the bottle and stared at its contents for a moment, then crossed himself. He poured a drink on Masha's grave and whispered. "I am sorry. I would have never shared our plans with you, had I known the out come."

"You!" Angrily snatching the bottle from his hand, I glared at him, and growled, "I wondered how."

He avoided looking at me. I turned my eyes towards the other two. They looked away. Chugging what was left, I dropped the bottle at Stefon's feet and walked back to the church.

CHAPTER TWO

Awake before the others, I lay on the cold stone floor. My gut burning from the vodka, I tried rubbing my stomach to make it feel better. All it did was force me to go outside and relieve myself.

Alone in the dark, all I could think about was the food in the back of the car. Finished peeing on a bush in the church yard, I stumbled thru the darkness to the car and pawed at the trunk latch until I got it open. Afraid of using any light out of fear it might be seen by somebody, I searched blindly through the boxes. Shaking each can my hand touched, if I liked the sound, in the moonlight, I held the label inches from my face guessing at the picture on it. Feeling a square tin, I held it up. There was no visable label. I shook it. "Ahh yes, the sound of loose leaf tea. Now for a can of fruit."

Holding up another can in the dim light, I could see white marbles in the label's picture. "Uhmm, pears...I think." I stuffed the tea and canned fruit under an arm. "May as well find some fish too. At least the flat cans make them an easy find." Feeling around, I found one and shoved it in my coat pocket. Randomly grabbing two more cans from another box, I stuffed them into my coat pockets.

Making an effort to be quiet inside the church, I knelt, placing the tins on the hearth. Opening the tea and taking whiff, I sighed with desire, then set about to revive the smoldering embers. Bent over the scattered coals and flicking them into a pile, I heard footsteps come up behind me. I could tell it was Katya. She stood there for a moment before speaking. "You found the food, good."

Ignoring her while blowing on the embers until a small flame popped up, I glanced at her as I reached for a twig. "What do you mean?"

"You found..." she stepped over my feet, "the boxes of food that were in the car. Yes?"

The fire being more important to me than an early morning conversation with her, I looked past her for something to put on the tiny flame. "Yeah."

Picking up a small spruce twig, she held it out to me. "You don't like me, do you?"

I took the twig and broke it into littler pieces. "I...it's not that I don't like you. It's more like...I don't want to fight with you."

She sat down on the floor. "You mean about Masha?"

Now, the cold morning air was not the only thing making me uncomfortable. "Yes, our relationship was..." bending over, I blew on the small flicker of a flame.

"She never told you?"

"Told me what? That her husband turned her in for subversion, then divorced her?" I started fanning the flame. "Or...that the furs were something to buy her way out?"

Katya picked up the tin containing the tea, turned it from side to side, then set it down. "I take it she never told you of her feeling towards you? Even though you are an American."

Surprised by her comment, I knocked the small fire out onto the stone floor with the piece of wood I was using for a fan. I bit my tongue, as I looked at the burning embers strewn about. In an attempt to keep from saying something stupid, I gave her a toothy grin.

Katya, pointing to the scattered ashes, asked, "You are an American, yes?"

I flicked the largest of the embers back together. "I'm a Gypsy from Germany, not American."

Katya cocked her head clicking her tongue. "OK, a gypsy that speaks American while making love?"

"Nyet!" I fanned the smoking pile of embers harder.

"You know... she asked Tomas if you were." Shaking the hair from her eyes, she grinned, "He told her that you were and demanded that she keep it a secret."

I gritted my teeth, refusing to look at her while trying to tease a flame once more from the blackened twigs. I had it ready to burst forth, when the smoke tickled my nose. Not turning away fast enough, I sneezed, blowing ashes around.

"Here," Katya wedged herself between me and the embers. "You're not doing it right. You must respect the flame." Within a minute she had a bright, crackling flame. Carefully, she laid more fuel on the fire and then sat back on her haunches. As the flames grew stronger she mumbled, "I was turned in for teaching the village children my people's traditions." Taking a pinch of tea leaves and sprinkling them over the flame, Katya brushed her fingers together. "My grandfather was a shaman and taught me many ways of the old."

"He did an excellent job, too," Arek said, as he came over and stood next to her.

Katya, leaning against him, rubbed her cheek on his leg. "Thank you, Arek. You are always so kind to me."

Fingering my jaw where she had slapped me the night before, I sniped, "That's cause he's afraid of your anger."

"Careful." She playfully shook her fist at me.

Arek stepped back. "He's right."

Katya swung her fist at his legs. "You better be careful, too."

Sitting up, Stefon stared at the fire. "Is the tea ready yet?"

I grabbed the can of pears. "We don't have any water, unless we use what's in these."

Katya silently rose to her feet and took hold of the bucket of bloody water left from washing Masha.

"What are you going to do with that?" I asked.

"Going to the river to get water."

"I'm not drinking from that filthy thing." Throwing her the kettle I had found in the car, I pointed towards the back of the church. "There's a spring flowing on the other side of the cemetery. It's got to be cleaner than the river."

Arek watched her go out the door. "I better go with her...for her protection."

"Uh-huh, sure thing." I pulled my shiv from its sheath and stabbed the top of the canned pears. "While you're at it, find out what she knows about the contents of the car. I think it's time to know if we can trust her."

Stefon came over to the fireplace and held his hands above the fire. "We have a car and a few furs. You don't trust her with that?"

Prying back the jagged lid, I shoved my shiv into one of the pieces of white fruit. "Zarkhov had a stash of goods in the trunk." I held the pear out to Stefon. "I think there's enough food in the back, to get us to the coast."

He wiped his hand on his pants before taking the peeled, golf-ball-sized tidbit. "Hmmm, the coast you say?" Nibbling on it as if it were an expensive delicacy, he held it aloft. "Hmmm...how I miss fresh food. Especially fish."

I stuck another piece of fruit with my shiv. "Then you have no problem going east, to the coast?" I stuffed the whole pear in my mouth. It was firm and crunchy, like an apple. But tasteless just like the rest of the food in this country. I looked at the label in the light from the fire. "Damn, that's not a pear, that's a dog gone potato." Stefon smiled and popped the rest of his in his mouth. I held out another one to him. "And not back to Poland?"

Brushing my offer aside, he took the can from my hand. "I was praying about that last night. And I had an epiphany." He poured a little of the juice from the can into a tin cup he had found earlier and swirled it about. "I was standing alongside a river... when I saw a sheet descend from heaven—"

Rolling my eyes, I grinned. "You mean like the one Saint Paul had?"

"Peter." He tossed the dirty rinse onto the floor, then poured the rest of the liquid from the potatoes into his cup. "Ahh, then you know of his vision and what I must do."

"I know of the saint's vision, but what does that have to do with you? Your goal has always been to free Poland from the Soviet shackle."

Stefon pointed at the fire. "Would you mind." Then inhaling deeply through his nose and stroking his beard he went on, "As a priest, I..." he paused, taking a sip, "I must do God's will and not my own. Well, last night, as we laid Masha to rest, I had to question my own motives."

"So you'll come to America with me?"

"Haw. Travel to the most heathenistic country in the world! That, my friend, would be a powerful missionary trial." He wiped his mouth with the back of his wrist. "No. There are many unsaved souls here in the east that need my help."

"And what do we need to be saved from, Priest?" Katya asked, stepping into the room. "The Ukrainians already tried that a century ago. Don't you recognize this place? It's what's left of one of your orthodox churches." She set her bucket of water next to the fireplace.

Stefon, calm as ever, looked her in the eye. "I am sorry for the misguided judgment that had been levied against you earlier."

Before she could respond, Arek stepped between them and held the pot out to

me. "She knows what's in the car."

"Great..." Taking the kettle, I wiped it dry before reaching over to place it on the fire, "we're in agreement to go east, then. Yes?"

Katya grabbed the pot from my hand. "Don't, you'll put the fire out."

Stepping back, I brushed my hands together and sneered, "You want to take over?"

Arek cleared his throat and shook his head.

"Fine." Bending over, I picked up the can of tea and handed it to her. "You seem to have a thing with fire. Would you mind making the tea? Pleassse."

She knelt on the hearth, bowing and whispering to the fire before gently giving it more fuel. The flames sprang upwards, growing quickly.

Sliding the teapot into the bed of coals, she sat back and looked at me. "My people are the Evenki, from the Amur Valley. We have learned to survive in the wilderness, because we understand that fire is our sister. Take care of her, and she will take care of you."

Silently mocking her, I motioned to Stefon to hand me one of the cans on the other side of his feet.

"Just as fish in the river," Katya went on, making a wavy motion with her hand, "she will feed you."

"The fish, OK, I can see..." Taking the can from Stefon, I stabbed it with my knife. "But what's all that got to do with making our tea?"

Arek sat down next to me, crossing his legs. "She's familiar with the Siberian cultures. I think she would be a great asset in our travels."

"Meaning?" Prying up the jagged metal lid, I glanced over at him. "Ooo, that's right. You've taken a shining to her." Seeing that there were apricots in the can, I grunted, "Uh-huh, sure, why not," and shoved them towards Arek.

After eating a meager breakfast of apricots, potatoes, and fish, Stefon clapped his hands together, announcing, "I, for one am tired of wearing this rag of a shirt. Shall we step out to the car and see what the Lord has proved?"

The expensive shirts and jackets that Zarkhov stole from prisoners weren't exactly designed for warmth, but at least they were in good condition, making us look more like travelers, than like escaped prisoners. Having found on the top of the pile a heavy shirt that fit me, I left the others to rummage through the boxes while I said goodbye to Masha one more time.

Picking up a small pebble along the path, I placed it on the pile of bricks at the head of her grave. It was becoming difficult to breathe as I stared at her grave through the mist in my eyes and the thoughts of having watched Tomas, my friend and brother, along with Masha, the love of my life, senselessly murdered on the same day. Falling to my knees, I looked up in the sky and screamed, "Why did they have to die? Why couldn't you have taken me and left them?"

Unable to hear an answer from the clouds, I wiped my face with my coat sleeve and looked at the pile of rubble covering Masha's grave. I crumbled, sprawling upon her grave crying her name over and over desperately wanting her to answer. In the silence that lives among the dead, I lost track of time; until Arek started the car.

Pushing myself to my knees, I picked up a second pebble, pressed it against my lips, then gently set it next to the first, "I will never forget you, Masha."

The others left me alone as we drove along the dirt road heading north and east to find the Trans-Siberian Highway. After making several wrong turns onto dead-end forest roads, we came to a wide hard-packed gravel road. Arek stopped the car, giving Katya a chance to study the crude drawing of a map.

A huge dump truck went by.

"Oh great," I whined. "A damn mining road. Where the hell is—"

Katya, leaning forward, dropped the folded paper onto the front seat beside me. "This is the highway."

"You gotta be kidding?" I turned, looking at her. "What are the petrol stations like, a broken down car on the side of the road with a hose sticking out of its gas tank?"

"In some cases, yes." She sat there with a pissed look on her face. Then knocking my elbow off the back of the seat, she snapped, "They're just like those in Europe. Idiot."

I raised my hand, flipping her off.

She tried grabbing my finger. "You need to lose your American ego. A gesture like that would give us away."

"Hey..." I wadded up a piece of paper, and threw it at her. "If it wasn't for this American, you'd still be back in that hell hole."

"She's right." Arek glanced past me as he turned onto the highway. "We need to find fuel right away. When we stop, we'll be in a Federal Security car and not dressed the part."

In an effort to be pragmatic, I blurted out, "OK, we dump the car and take a train. At least then I could be a tourist sleeping in a comfortable bed. Oooh hell yes, that would be better than driving these damn dirt roads"

Katya kicked the back of my seat. "An American tourist with no papers, that's smart."

"Fine! You got a better—" I stiff-armed the dash. "Watch out!"

Arek hit the brakes too late, everyone's head hit the roof as the car bounced through the pot-hole.

"Damn." Gingerly, I touched the top of my head. "Pull over. Now I gotta pee."

Arek let the car roll to a stop. I bailed out and sprinted for the closest bush. While relieving myself, I took a cigarette from my pocket and lit it. After I had finished watering the bush and zipped up, I stood there staring off into the woods. Finally, stretching my arms, the cold air helped clear my head making the walk back pleasant.

Arek was underneath the car inspecting the steering mechanism while Katya leaned against the fender next to his feet glaring at me as she puffed on a cigarette. Stefon stood next to his open door, staring down the road. Patting the roof of the car, I asked, "Hey Stefon, you want to hold a prayer service for it?"

Katya flicked her cigarette at me. "Shut up, smart-ass." Pushing off the car, she walked over to Stefon and gazed down the road, too.

Stefon ran his fingers through his thick black hair as he turned, placing his elbows on the roof of the car. "One of us will have to put on Zarkhov's uniform. It's the only way."

"Ha..." I raised both my hands in protest. "Not me! I barely speak the language."

Katya bumped Stefon. "He couldn't even pass for a drunk peasant."

I flipped her the finger.

"See what I mean, he's so unfamiliar with their ways."

Stefon nodded in agreement.

Arek slid out from under the car. "I'll do it. Zarkhov was taller than Kezel...more my size." He wiped his dirty greasy hands on his trousers. "Besides, it would look better if the driver was the one with the uniform. That's my opinion."

"Thank you, Arek." Shoving my hands in my pockets, I rocked back and forth on my heels. "I was just about to suggest that."

Katya picked up a stone.

Stefon seized her wrist. "Don't!"

Sneering at Katya, I smacked the back of my hand in the palm of my other, mocking her as I spoke in English, "Momma mia...you-a betta watcha you self." Walking to the back of the car I pulled out the bloody uniform, "The thing is nasty, it needs to be washed." I held it up. "That'll give her something to do."

"That should be your job," Stefon said as he retrieved the teapot from the trunk. "She has to make something for us to eat, while Arek and I change the flat tire."

Arek stopped wiping his hands. "What flat tire?"

Stefon kicked the tire he had been leaning next to. "This one." Holding out the pot to Katya, he grinned, "Please?"

I dropped the coat back into the trunk. "Wrong person for the job."

Stefon rarely used his size to get his way. Instead, he always glared at me like he was trying to light a prayer candle. I bit my lip and wadded up the uniform, then followed Katya towards a stream about a hundred meters from the road.

Tripping over a vine growing across the path, I muttered, "Why am I, ouch,...I don't know how to get blood out. Not without using soap. Besides it's a woman's job to wash clothes."

Katya stopped in her tracks, keeping her back to me. "You're damn right. A woman could do anything better than you." Pushing a limb aside, she continued walking through the brush.

"Really?" I reached out to stop the thin whip of a limb and missed it. "Ouch, damn it. Then how come I'm the one that got us out?"

Throwing one leg over a log laying across the path and straddling it, she stared off into the brush for a few seconds. Then cocking her head to one side, she swung back around. "Me and Masha would have gotten out one way or another."

I stood there dumbstruck at her self-assurance as she walked away. Then it dawned on me what she meant. I leaped over the log and trotted up seizing her by the arm. "I should have known."

"Known what?" she asked, as she stopped at the edge of the stream.

"That you were jealous of Masha and me being together."

I wrapped my arms around her.

"Let go of me."

Leaning back, I looked at her with one eye closed. She sucker-punched me. Staggering back, I slipped on some wet rocks and fell into the shallow pool of water. Before I could get to my feet, she pulled her knife from its hiding spot and shoved it under my chin. "You ever touch me again, I'll cut your throat, ear to ear."

"Whoa." I held up my hand, gently pushing her knife away. "My mistake. I got the wrong impression."

"You thought, I...wanted you?" She laughed as she put the knife away. "Arek's right, you Americans are so damn self-centered. You think the world revolves around you."

"You..." I stood up, "and Arek, really are?"

She nodded.

"He never said anything to me and Stefon, other than you two were friends."

Katya recovered the tea kettle floating along the edge of the stream. Wading into the middle of the knee-deep pool, she bent over to fill it.

Moaning and gripping her stomach, she started to tumble head first into the water. Jumping over and latching onto her coat, I managed to keep her from going in.

Jerking free, she dropped to her hands and knees with her face a mere hair's thickness above the water and dry heaved several times.

"You OK?"

Glaring at me through the wet hair plastered to her face, she dragged a coat sleeve across her mouth.

That was enough to answer my question.

Splashing water onto her face, then slowly rising, she arched her back. "You say a word to Arek and I'll—"

"I know...you'll cut my throat. I take it he doesn't know."

Bending over, bracing her hands on her knees, she looked at her own reflection. "We need him to be strong and focused until we can get some place safe."

Zarkov's jacket bumped her leg as it tried to float by. I reached for it, "Whoa, almost lost—"

Katya lashed out grabbing my coat and held tight. "Promise me!"

If there was one thing I had just learned; women could be ruthless and if I wanted to survive... I looked her in the eye, "I promise."

CHAPTER THREE

Our first night driving on the Trans-Siberian Highway taught us why few people drove it in the dark. It was difficult spotting the potholes until too late, giving everyone whiplash and headaches. And, since there were so few other drivers, along with no dividers in the middle of the road, everyone traveled all over the graveled road searching for that smooth path.

The second time Arek plowed into the ditch avoiding a collision, nobody argued with his demanding to travel only during the daylight. "That way," he ranted, "we can avoid the truck stops and buy our fuel from peddlers on the side of the road. The only thing they ask is, 'Let's see the money.' They don't care about no ration card."

Not wanting to give up on the petrol stations, I looked back at Stefon. "Hmm, I for one, don't know about that part. But having Zarhkov's ID and ration card, it gives us a discount on fuel."

Arek tossed Zarhkov's papers into my lap. "I might look like him in the dark, but really, in full daylight? I'm not willing to take that chance again. The last attendant demanded to see my travel papers. Then he got cocky and wasn't going to give me back the ration card until I convinced him the station would get a late night visit if he didn't hand it over."

Holding up Zarhkov's picture, I compared the two. "OK, I see your point. But I think Katya should do the bargaining with the roadside sellers from now on." Handing Arek the papers, I glanced back at Katya. She was chewing on her knuckles and curled her nose at me. Grinning, I turned forward. "Beside, she's the only one who doesn't have a foreign accent."

* * *

By mid-morning of the third day and finding no gasoline peddlers on the side of the road, we decided to take a chance at the next filling station. Stefon, in the middle of the discussion, pointed out, "We could purchase some other supplies and fresh bread. That would make everything look—"

Arek shook his head, "I don't—"

"Hear me out brother." Stefon reached up placing his hand on Arek's shoulder. "I've been praying about it. The plan would be for me and Kezel to stay in the car, while you, in Zarhkov's uniform, pumped the fuel. Katya, would go inside, shop for food...but not pay for it until she saw you were done. Then she'll go to the cashier, ask how much for the fuel and the food. If she's questioned about the ration card, she'll say she's your wife, drop a few extra Rubles on the counter and leave."

Katya, brushing her hair out of her face, looked at him. "What happens if they should demand I stop and return to the counter?"

"Stop...but without looking back, politely ask something like...are you demanding a larger gratuity? If you are, my husband, Major Zarhkov of state security, will have a chat with you while he is on the phone to headquarters explaining why we are late."

Stefon's plan worked without a hitch. It worked so good, the locals encountered at the pumps also gave us a clear berth as soon as they saw the uniform stepping from the car. Arek began to enjoy the masquerade and soon started passing up the peddlers just so we had to stop at gas stations.

The highway, leaving its path along the river, crossed over a mountain and entered an isolated valley. Heavily timbered with pine and spruce, the trees grew right up to the edge of the road creating a shadowy netherworld where shafts of sunshine caused momentary white-outs on the windshield. Slowing down, Arek rubbed at the dirty glass with his hand. "We have anything to clean this with?"

Reaching under the seat, I pulled out an oily rag. "How about this?"

"Be careful, Arek." Katya leaned forward putting a hand on his shoulder. "Robbers like areas like this. They'll drop trees across the road, knowing you won't be able to see them."

The words weren't anymore than out of her mouth, when we passed a sign indicating there was a station not far up the road. Arek pulled over and held out his hand, palm up.

I looked at him. "What? You want the rag?"

"The revolver and holster."

I twisted my mustache, heckling him. "Planning on robbing the place, huh?"

"I need to look fierce in these parts, and Chekists are always armed." He wiggled his fingers, "Give me the gun."

Stefon, who had spent most of the day with his eyes closed praying, spoke up rather forcefully. "No more killing."

I didn't move. "What's a Chekist?"

Katya jumped at the chance to defend Arek. "He's right. Its part of their uniform and he'll need it. Give it to him."

"OK, OK, I don't care if he wants to wear the damn thing." Reaching under the seat, I pulled out the handgun. "I was just askin' what the fuck's a Chekist."

Stefon sat up repeating louder, "No more killing."

"Damn it, Stefon," Arek growled. "I'm only wearing the uniform, not becoming one of them."

Katya screeched, "Give 'em the gun."

"No!" Stefon growled.

Arek punched the accelerator throwing us back into our seats as the car fishtailed across the graveled highway.

"Whoa." I grabbed hold of the dash. "You won't need the gun to kill somebody if you're gunna keep driving like this."

He backed his foot off the pedal.

I growled while clearing my throat and was about to make a snide comment, when he stretched his neck from side to side. My last ride with Herman in Berlin, flashed before my eyes. Ignoring everyone, Arek pulled into the station and slipped it into neutral, letting the car roll through the empty lot while he glanced around. As it rolled by the farthest pump from the roadhouse, he stopped.

I held the pistol out to him. "Here ya go cowboy."

Taking it, he stepped out of the car, and with a flare of arrogance strapped it on. Then pulling smooth his knee-length leather coat, he took a wad of rubles from his pocket and handed them through the open window to Katya.

She nodded and winked.

I held a few more folded notes over the seat to her. "Cigarettes."

Taking the money, she unlatched her door. "What kind?"

Out of habit I replied, "Marlboro."

Ignoring me, she quietly counted the money in her hands before folding the bills. "Stefon?"

He smiled. "I will be happy with whatever you get."

Katya got out and hurried to the disheveled wooden building.

I watched her enter, then looked at Stefon over the seat, "What's a Chekist?"

Looking down, he pinched his belly. "Hmm, I've lost a lot of weight this last year."

"We all have." I looked around the empty lot. "You're avoiding my question."

The car rocked a little as he twisted and stretched his shoulders. "They are the secret enforcers of the Soviet power. They are the ones who show up in the middle of the night. Or at your job..." he paused, massaging his eyes. "Their job... is making people disappear. They all wear the same leather coat, like what Arek has on."

Looking at the coat, I remembered something about the reference in Zarkhov's file. "That would explain why Zarkhov was—"

Arek knock on the side of the car interrupting me.

We both looked at him as he pointed towards the large glass window of the wooden roadhouse.

Katya could be seen inside, flailing her arms about as she spoke to the woman behind the counter. Jumping out of the car, I reached for the nozzle. "Go check it out. I'll finish pumping."

Arek tugged on his leather coat and pulled the brim of his hat down over his eyes as he walked towards the door. At the entrance, he whistled, pointing to a stack of empty fuel cans next to the step.

Clicking off the hose, I ran over to the stack of cans. Their large handles made it awkward to hang onto four while running back to the car. Stumbling, I dropped them in the dirt next to the car as Stefon jumped out to help. He had just placed the third one in the trunk when Katya burst out the station's door. She was half-shoving, half-dragging the woman from inside, towards the car.

Arek, quickly following them out the door, carried three large bags of food. I spilt petrol on my foot at the sight of what was going down. "Damn it. Stefon, throw me a rag."

He didn't hear a word, he had already ran over and took two of the bags from Arek.

Shutting the pump off, I dropped the hose on the ground and hurriedly put the last can into the trunk then jumped into the front seat.

Katya slammed the woman head-first against the car. Jerking open the door, she shoved the woman into the back seat before climbing in beside her. The woman screaming incoherently, opened the door on the other side, trying to scramble out. Stefon, waiting for someone to open the door, quickly slid in foiling her escape. Arek, heaving the bag in his hands onto the front seat between us, climbed in behind the wheel.

Flying out of the station in a controlled sideways drift across the graveled highway, I yelled at Arek over the noise coming from the backseat. "What the fuck's going on?"

"She wanted—" Arek grimaced at the shrill noise coming from the two women. "Shut-up, both of you." His angry voice proved quite effective. Both women shut up and stared at him. "The proprietor's clan are ancestral enemies with Katya's people. She claimed if an Evenki has any rubles, they must have been stolen." He glanced at me. "Then she demanded double the price or she'd call the authorities."

"So..." I blinked at him, "everything a Chekist has, is stolen. Why didn't you pay the price?"

"Too late," he glanced at the outside mirror. "By the time I got there she had already dialed."

Riled about the sudden complications, I hissed while glancing back at our unwanted passenger. Grinding my teeth, I pulled the bag of food a little closer to me. "Didn't Katya point out that, as a Chekist, you, were the authority?"

Stefon, pulling a package of shoe laces from one of his bags, looked at the laces. "So what do you plan we do with her?"

Arek shrugged. "I don't know."

"Tie her to a tree for the wolves," Katya snarled as she reached over snatching the laces from his hands. Opening the package, she wrapped one around the woman's wrists. "That's what they did to my people."

Stefon recited his previous demand. "No...more...killing."

"She's already called the authorities," I shrugged. "We don't have a choice."

"I forbid it," Stefon bellowed. "We cannot become monsters like Zarkhov."

"You forbid it," I shrieked. "Who the fuck—"

Katya hit me in the head with her elbow. My head bounced off the door window. "Damn it, woman."

"Watch your mouth." Katya finished tying the laces around her prisoner's wrists. "You need to show the priest more respect."

"Arek..." I rubbed my head, not sure what to do. "We got a damn tiger back there. Can't you do something about her?"

"A beautiful tiger, at that." Arek smiled as he looked at her in the mirror. Taking a deep breath, he tapped the wheel, "She's right, tho. We're not in the camps anymore, you need to be more careful of what you say."

I sat back staring out the window. Katya's reflection was in the glass. I tried looking through her image as she put a cover over the woman's head. With her enemy now blindfolded, she sat back and stared at Arek while chewing on her knuckles. His foot was heavy on the accelerator as we barreled down the highway in silence.

The four of us, content with it being that way. Katya's prisoner, however, decided otherwise. She started babbling, "I'm going to be missed when the police show up. You know they will come looking for me."

At first, everyone tried ignoring her.

Then she spewed a new threat. "My son is a policeman, he will come looking for me. He comes by every day, and when he sees I'm not there, he'll find me."

Katya mumbled, "Shut up."

"I'm also the chairwoman of the local transportation committee. And I will be missed at our weekly meeting this afternoon."

Fed up with her noise, I looked over at Stefon rolling my eyes.

He nodded, pinching the end of his nose. "Of course you will be, madam."

"Good," she snapped. "Then you'll let me out. Now!"

Stefon leaned forward. "Yes ma'am. As soon as we can find a safe spot to pull over." He tapped Arek on the shoulder and pointed to a side road coming up ahead.

Arek slowed down and turned.

Once we were out of sight from the highway, Stefon declared, "Here!"

As the car rolled to a stop, Stefon opened his door. "Yes, madam, you are important to God too." With the hood still over her head, he gently helped her out of the car. "This way please."

Stefon guided the babbling woman to a birch tree and bound her arms loosely around it. Before walking away, he said a prayer. She cursed him the whole time. Returning to the car with a smile on his face, Stefon slid in and quietly pulled the door shut. "See, no one has to die."

Opening my mouth to make an objection, Katya stopped me by shoving her finger in my face and giving me that look, warning of impending pain. Turning back around, I shook my head as Arek pulled out onto the highway.

Katya broke the silence, "If it's any consolation, Kezel, there is about a one percent chance of her being found in the next couple of days. And I doubt anyone will believe her story that she was kidnapped."

I hit the dashboard with disapproval of how things were done and said nothing. The friction between the three of us kept things quiet while we continued to barrel down the highway. Out of boredom, I reached over twisting the radio knob in search of a station, hoping to be somewhere else, other than in this car. The speaker hissed nothing but empty static. The only thing left was watching the sporadic changes of scenery; open meadows dotted with trees, then thick forest, then open meadows....

Towards dark, Arek pulled in to a meadow alongside the highway, saying he needed to take a break. I bailed out. Walking into the middle of the tall grass, I lit a cigarette. Working my frustration out on a clump of grass, I finished my smoke before walking back to the car. Stefon had brought wood over from the other side of the highway giving Katya material to built a fire in front of the car. Arek had the four gas cans out on the ground and started wrestling with the boxes of food. "Good you're back, take this one up to Katya, will you please?"

Balancing the heavy box of canned goods on the edge of the trunk, I looked at the feeble condition of the box, "What's going on?"

"Katya's making the evening meal and she's decided we're spending the night here."

I shoved the box back in the trunk. Grabbing three cans, I sniped, "This is all she needs."

CHAPTER FOUR

The next morning, getting off to a poor start. We couldn't find enough dry wood to do more than heat water for tea and to melt the ice off the frozen ham Arek had snagged during the roadhouse fiasco. As the water was heating, Katya wanted to drop some of the canned potatoes into it. After giving her a few choice words about ruining my tea, her face turned red and she ran to the trunk, popping the lid open. Following her, I watched her grab a sweater out of the trunk and bury her face in it trying to hide a bout of the dry heaves from Arek and Stefon as they tried scraping the thick frost off the windshield with cardboard.

In the process of turning the car around, the tires couldn't grip the frozen grass, forcing me and Stefon to get out and push. Out on the road our luck didn't improve much. The graveled surface with its ruts from the heavy trucks, was frozen solid. It seemed like we could feel every pebble on its surface.

By late morning, the weather warmed up enough to melt the road into a slippery mess. Burning through fuel faster than usual and no gas station in sight, we stopped along the side of the road to pore the spare cans into the tank.

While Arek and I transferred the fuel, Stefon and Katya went for a short walk in the woods in search of mushrooms. Setting the first empty can down on the ground, Arek laughed, "I hope no one stops thinking we're selling it."

Leaning against the car door next him, I twisted, stretching my back. "You know Arek,...I sure hope you know what you're getting into with her."

He rattled the can in an effort to loosen the pour spout. "What do you mean?"

"She's...well..."

"She's what?" Katya asked, stepping past me, putting her arms around Arek.

The sound of a truck coming around the curve in the highway stopped me from answering.

It barely got past us, when the driver anchored its brakes, sliding to a stop. The tanker truck and trailer slowly backed up.

Arek tossed the empty can in his hands to the ground.

The driver rolled down his window as the big rig came to a halt. Tapping his fingers on the steering wheel, he sat in the cab staring at the three of us. Arek pulled Zarhkov's coat from the trunk and put it on. After he had buttoned the last button, the driver asked, "Having car troubles?"

Crossing his arms, Arek looked up at him. "Nope, just putting petrol in the car."

Picking up the empty can, I carried it around to the back of the car. The driver shifted in his seat and glanced at his far-side mirror. "You need more petrol? I have a few extra liters."

"How much?" Arek asked.

"Seventy-five kopecks."

Katya, grabbing Arek's arm, howled, "That's robbery!"

"Quiet, woman," Arek snapped as he kept his eyes on the driver. "Thirty-five."

The trucker, changing his focus to Katya, had an odd grin on his face. "Seventy-five."

Arek tugged on his jacket sleeve. "Forty-five."

The trucker sneered as he shook his head.

Arek, putting his hand behind his back, countered, "That's more than double the going price."

"Seventy-five," the driver repeated, not taking his eyes off Katya. His sudden interest in her made me nervous.

Arek slid his hand onto the revolver strapped to his side. "Maybe I should just shoot you and claim you tried to rob us. Then I could take all I want."

The trucker leaned further out his window, motioning towards me and Katya. "You won't shoot with these two around. Seventy-five."

"You're awful sure of yourself." Arek took several steps away from Katya, loosening the strap over the pistol. "You know as well as I, that robberies on this road are common. Fifty."

"You're not from around here, are you?"

"What does that matter? I have the authority—"

"That's what I thought." The trucker laid his chin on his bicep, gazing at Katya. "I know she's from around—."

"Duh!" I blurted out. "We're in Asia and she's Asian."

Katya pulled her knife from her coat sleeve. "You don't know me! And don't you compare me with road trash like yourself."

"Ahh, Katya," he grinned. "You haven't changed at all. I knew it was you when I drove by."

With a puzzled look on her face, she lowered her knife.

Raising his head off his arm, he chuckled, "You still have that scar on your left butt cheek?"

I looked at Arek and could see we were both lost as to what to make of his question. Taking a step towards her, Arek wasn't fast enough. A smile burst across her face as she screamed, "Vasiy!"

The driver, kicking open his door, jumped down and she ran into his out stretched arms. "It's good to see you again, Little Tiger."

Tears were rolling down her face. "I've missed you, Vasiy."

Glancing over at Arek again, I really didn't know what to think now. His hand, still on the pistol, also had an uncertainty showing in his stance.

Katya, finally releasing her grip on the trucker, turned towards us. "Arek, this is my mother's-sister's-son; Vasiy Kalinen. The big brother that I always looked up to."

Arek, taking his hand off the revolver, walked over to them. "What made you so sure I wouldn't shoot?"

Gripping Arek's hand, he shrugged, "I've been picked up by the police enough times to know a real one." Letting go, he reached behind his seat and pulled out an end-cap to the delivery pipe under the large fuel tanks. The cap had a garden hose valve fitted into it. Handing the modified cap to Arek, he opened the truck door further and reached inside. A pistol hung from the door's arm rest. "Besides, I had mine pointed at you the whole time. You never would have gotten yours out of the holster."

Not thrilled with her cousin's manner of introduction, he seemed a little too cocky towards Arek to suit me, I picked up two of our empty gas cans and shook them in an attempt to distract the conversation. "How far is it to the Pacific Ocean?"

Vasiy walked to the back of his trailer and connected the special cap onto the tanks' drain pipe. As the gasoline flowed into our can, he looked up at me. "Why, you planning on swimming some where?"

I dropped the other can next to his toes. "No. We're gunna walk over the ice."

Letting gas spill all over the can and onto the ground next to my feet, Vasiy glanced at his cousin. "Katya, where did you find these foreign nut cakes?"

"I'm not exactly little any more," she grabbed Arek's arm, squeezing it. "They helped me escape."

"Uhmm. On the road I heard something about a prison riot put-down. Were you involved?"

She lowered her eyes and tapped the overflowing fuel can with her shoe. "You might say that. We...we need a place to hide." She perked up, giving him a pleading look, "Is grandfather's cabin still there?"

Vasiy's smile faded. Twisting the valve, he shut off the flow of petrol. "The committee had it torn down after he disappeared."

Trying not to step into the spilt fuel, I dropped another empty can beside him and carefully switched the hose. He turned the valve on, then arched his back. "Vlad's cabin will be empty this winter. He fell off the roof and broke several bones. But, it should already be well stocked."

Stefon, stepping from his hiding spot behind a thick cedar, began picking his way through the bramble of thorny vines. "Would there be enough provisions for four?"

Vasiy didn't look up from his filling the cans. "I was wondering when you were going to come out." He jerked the hose from one can as liquid boiled out the opening, and thrust it into a waiting empty one. "The cabin is big enough for two, may..ay..be three." He looked at Stefon. "But not four."

I dropped an empty can at his feet. "Don't worry about us, we're used to a tight squeeze." Shaking my head at seeing how much fuel was on the ground, I reached over picking up a full one. "I think—"

Stefon cut me short. "That's what I thought." He stepped off the bank onto the road pulling at a thorn caught in his beard. "If that is the case we'll go through provisions too fast."

"You remember the valley where we used to play?" He glanced up at Katya while bent over the fuel cans. "The old babushka's cabin?"

She nodded, stepping away from the splashing petrol.

"The old woman is still there. I deliver kerosene and groceries to her once a month."

At the sound of a car approaching on the highway Vasiy shut off the flow of gasoline. Arek dropped the can in his hand and walked to the rear of the truck's trailer, making himself visible to the oncoming car. Pretending he had paper and pencil in his hands, he twisted, watching the car's approach. As it drew close, the car quickly sped up and flew by.

Vasiy picked up the hose, letting it dangle as he spoke. "Her hut is just over the ridge from Vlad's. I could leave you supplies with her."

Katya stepped away from the dripping hose. "What about the local committee? Won't they get suspicious?"

Stuffing the end of the hose in one of the cans, he turned the valve on again. "No one bothers her. They claim she's possessed...I think the committee's hoping she'll die this winter."

"She's not sick, is she?"

"No," Vasiy laughed. "Don't you remember how she is?" Nodding at Arek, he whispered, "Just make sure she doesn't see that coat. Or you'll find out how powerful her medicine really is."

With the last can and car full, Vasiy shut the drain valve off, allowing the last four or five liters in the pipe to flow onto the ground. Tossing the special cap into the cab, he pulled a rag from the door pocket and began speaking to Katya in their native tongue as he wiped his hands.

Pawing through the clothes in the trunk, Stefon held a silk shirt up against me hindering my placing the last can of gasoline in the trunk. "Look at this, won't even fit you. What was Zarkhov thinking?" he grumbled. Snatching a thick sweater way too small for himself, he held it out for a second then threw it back into the box and slammed the trunk lid shut. Stepping from behind the car, Stefon became animate with his frustration as he approached Vasiy. "I need to find some larger cloths. What we have is too small for me. Look at these rags...I'm afraid I'm not adequately dressed for the winter. Can you get me some?"

With a big grin, Vasiy nodded. "I can get you anything you want, but it'll take time. In the meantime, ask the old woman. Her husband was about your size."

Katya pulled a wad of paper money from her pocket. Pressing it into her cousin's hand, she hugged him. "Thank you. It's so good to see family again."

Taking the cash, he stuffed it in his pocket and then ruffled her hair. "I'll tell your mother that you're OK." Tossing the rag in his hand behind his seat, he climbed into the rig. "However, the papers will take some time."

Opening the trunk, I grabbed several of the watches from the box of jewelry. "You need a few things for payment?"

The truck's engine spit black smoke as it rumbled to life. Leaning out his window he grinned, "Watches? They gotta be stolen." He gave me a thumb's up as he let out the clutch. "Keep 'em. They'll come in handy later."

I could barely hear him over the roar of the engine. But at that point it didn't matter. We had a destination, and a place to hide. The stress of escaping from a Soviet prison, seemed, as Stefon claimed; To have been lifted by provenance.

Katya carried on non-stop for the next hour about her childhood as we drove down the highway. While telling us, that Vasiy, the oldest male child in her extended family, had been like an older brother to her and her two younger sisters, a military truck roared past us going the other way. Her voice quickly faded away.

Looking at her reflection in the window, I saw Stefon place his hand on her shoulder. With a melancholy look out the window she continued, "As the oldest, he was the first in our family to get conscripted. We were proud of him. He made rank fast, until Moscow sent him to Czechoslovakia to put down their uprising." She wadded up the coat in her lap, hugging it. "He came back disillusioned with the Soviet system and has been living on the fringe since."

Stefon mumbled, " It's OK."

With tears on her cheeks, Katya continued staring out the window. "Damn them."

Sighing, Stefon patted her on the arm. "I remember that spring very vividly. I was fresh from training when my unit was sent to Prague, also. We were ordered to intimidate the Czechs by any means possible. To quash any desire they had to improve their lives."

"I was lucky." Arek looked at his Polish brother in the rear view mirror. "I was sent to the border where we waited for orders that never came."

Clueless to what they were referring to, I eyed Stefon. "What invasion are you guys talking about? The war was over in forty-five. Way before you were born."

"It was..." Stefon snapped his fingers, "August of nineteen sixty-eight. Moscow did not want to lose its grip on Prague."

"Sixty-eight!" I took a long hard look at him. "How old are you?"

Touching   his   fingers   together,   Stefon   counted, "Twenty-five...six...twenty-seven, I believe."

I looked at Arek. "And?"

"Twenty-eight, next week."

"Damn, I'm hanging around with a bunch of old farts." I started laughing. "No wonder my joints ache and I need a cane."

Katya reached over the seat, trying to twist my ear. "What about you? How old are you?"

I jerked free of her hand. "Old enough to know how to snag the front seat for a week."

"OK, smart-ass." She snatched a bottle of water from the seat next to Stefon. "How old are you?"

Howling, "OK, OK." I leaned forward trying to get away from the chilled wetness running down my back. "Twenty last time I counted. What about you?"

"None of your business," she snapped dumping more water down my back.

"What the hell was that for?" I arched my back trying to escape the water's stinging chill.

Katya's actions got Stefon laughing so hard, tears rolled down his face.

Arek slowed the car down in his effort to wipe the tears from his eyes. "Haven't you learned yet, not to ask a woman her age?"

I reached over the seat offering her my hand. "Touche! My mistake."

Katya shoved my arm out of the way. Leaning over the seat, she tapped Arek on the shoulder and pointed down the road. "Take the next left. On the other side of that bridge," she motioned to the left. "There's the road that will take us to the cabin."

CHAPTER FIVE

The narrow dirt road through the wooded mountains was treacherous going. At times barely wide enough for the car, the track often dropped into little hollows where Arek would have to race through the muck of a seep. For what seemed like hours, he struggled to keep the car moving. Finally, we came to a small meadow. Katya leaned over the back of the front seat and pointed out into it. "Keep following the road."

Not far into the grassy field, she pointed at what looked like two parallel cow trails taking off from the road, running through the middle of the tall grass towards a wooded gully. In the beginning, shadows cast by the tall grass, kept the muddy tracks frozen and gave the tires something to grip. As we slowly progressed, the tracks turned so that the sun touched the ground melting the frost, making a slippery mess.

Once we were able to get across the meadow and into the timber, the little used road had enough forest litter frozen to its surface to provide traction. The tracks continued through the forest for close to a kilometer, where a large tree lay across the road blocking further access.

Getting out, I asked, "Anybody remember if there's an axe in the back?"

Katya hurriedly stepped from the car and popped open the trunk. "We have to walk the rest of the way."

I turned around looking beyond the log. "You gotta be kidding?"

"No. Vlad dropped the tree here on purpose. It's meant to discourage people from going any further."

Stefon, trying to pick up one of the boxes of canned goods, fumbled with it till the bottom tore loose. "Phhf, how far is it, you say?"

Katya, reached in the trunk, taking a long-sleeved shirt from the clothing pile and tied knots in its sleeves. "Not far, just down the path a ways." She slid as many cans in the sleeves as she could, then threw the shirt over her shoulder.

Picking up a shirt from the pile, I held it up, it was short sleeved. "How far is, not far? Five minutes... an hour?"

"Oh, I don't know..." she tied another shirt in knots. "Maybe thirty minutes."

Arek grabbed four shirts. "She's got a good idea, there." He handed two to Stefon. "At that distance,we couldn't make it back for a second load before dark."

Each of us loaded as much food and clothing as we could over our shoulders. Getting ready to close the trunk lid, I mumbled, "Wait a minute," and grabbed the rifle along with a box of ammo.

Arek, seeing me do that, put his hand out. "Wait!... I've decided to strap on the pistol. Where's it at?"

Stefon, looking in the trunk as Arek moved things around in search of shells for the pistol, snatched the tea kettle and waved it to Katya, standing on the other side of the log waiting.

Hiking along the overgrown road, we soon came to a washout. Katya slid down the embankment and hopped over the small trickle of water to the other side. "It's not far from here."

Silently, the three of us men followed her lead climbing up the other side of the wash where the road disappeared into an over-growth of bramble. By the time I got to the top, Katya had pushed her way through the brush following a slightly noticeable trail. There was no way for the three of us, not to know which direction to go as she rambled on in a loud voice giving us a non-stop lesson on Evenki trappers and how well they keep their cabins stocked. Listening to her drivel about the fun she had as a child at the cabin during the summer, made my shoulders ached from their burden. Her prattle, along with the occasional slap from a limb, or slip in the mud, gave me the strong desire to cuddle up to a warm fire with a bottle in my hand.

The full moon, hanging in the tree tops, carved up the darkness under the trees by the time the cabin came into view. The rough-hewn log cabin was built into a steep hillside amongst a grove of evergreen trees. The bitter chill from a forest breeze made me forget about the bottle and kept me focused on building a fire while climbing the steps.

Stefon, pushing the door open, went in first. Arek followed close behind. Still on the steps, I heard the priest trip in the dark, cursing as he dropped his load of canned goods. Arek, hitting whatever it was, too, went sprawling in the darkness. Katya had the same idea as I, and we lit our cigarette lighters at the same time. The flames revealed our comrades' unfortunate situation, along with a lantern sitting on a table and a wood stove at the other end of the room. Dropping my bundle in the doorway, I went straight for the wood stove. Katya headed for the lantern.

The makings for a fire were already laid in the iron stove, all I had to do was put a match to the paper. Meanwhile, Katya, lighting the kerosene lantern, hung it from the hook in the center of the room.

From the light of the lantern, I sat down on the wood pile beside the stove surveying our hideout. The single room cabin was, maybe, at best five-by-eight meters. There were two bunks with drawers under them; one against the wall on each side of the stove. A small table was at the end of one bed, and a counter with a built-in basin was at the end of the other bed. On the counter next to the basin sat a wooden bucket.

The pail, catching my attention, I picked it up. It didn't have the stinging acrid odor I expected. "Who made the reservations for this place? There's no indoor plumbing!"

Katya opened one of the drawers and looked through it. "The toilet's down the path. And if you're not careful, I'll lock you in it."

"Fine," I dropped the bucket and unzipped my pants. "I'll just fill this in here then."

She tossed a flashlight from the drawer at me. "Follow the path at the bottom of the steps. Our water is the small spring twenty meters to the left of the trail, across from the outhouse. I doubt even you could miss that."

Returning to the small cabin, it was warm enough to take off my wet muddy clothes and hang them on the clothesline next to everyone else's. Wrapping in a warm blanket and exhausted, I stretched out on the wooden plank floor next to the wall. Even in my T-shirt and shorts under a thin blanket, it was the warmest I'd been since that fateful day in Ulm. Memories of life in Germany danced on the backside of my eyelids while my body melted into a pile on the floor.

* * *

The next morning, Stefon flipped my blanket off me with his foot. "Good morning, my friend. Tea?" He held a cup down low.

Eyes closed, I pawed around for the blanket ignoring him. In my stupor, I heard Katya and Arek talking about bacon, eggs, oatmeal, and orange juice. Finding the blanket, I mumbled, "Wake me when they're ready," and curled up with the blanket, pulling it over my head.

Stefon set the cup next to me and walked away.

Katya, shaking the floor as she jumped up, snatched the blanket, opened the door and threw it on the porch. Frosty cold air swept in, stinging my bare skin.

Scooting across the floor, I kicked the door shut. "Damn it. I'm awake. OK?"

Arek pulled the blankets on his bunk out of my reach. "It's about time."

Slowly sitting against a wall, I asked, "What time is it?"

"Almost noon."

I stood up, stretching in an effort to touch the ceiling. "Why didn't you wake me earlier? We need to get everything from the car."

Stefon, sitting on a crate next to the table blowing at the steam rising from his mug of tea, chuckled, "We've already done that while you were asleep."

I glanced around. There wasn't much room left with everything from the car scattered on the cabin floor. "Is there a shed outside to put stuff in?"

"That's not the issue," Arek said, shaking his head. "With or without a shed, it's going to be crowded with the five of us."

Startled at his comment, I looked at Katya. Her stony glare warning me, I asked, "What are you talking about? Is Katya's momma moving in with us?"

Stefon stirred his tea while looking at me with a pious expression. "There's no room at the inn for me and you, my friend. We need to move on. Or, we could build onto this cabin."

Grabbing my pants from the line and a large piece of fire wood from the wood-box, I slipped them on then sat on the chunk of wood. Seeing Katya's cigarettes on the table, I reached over, pilfered one and lit it. In the dimly lit cabin, it wasn't hard to imagine I was at a sidewalk cafe considering my choices. *Let's see...I could spend the winter snowed in somewhere, in who knows what kind of shelter with Stefon. Or...meander through a foreign country as a wanted criminal who had no documents as Katya has pointed out. Or...add onto this cabin.*

I gritted my teeth, twisting my mustache as I looked at each of the them. "I dunno..."

Arek, always the optimistic one, got up from the table. "I think we can do it. I checked..." he high-stepped over several piles of clothes and reached for the teapot, "all the tools we need are here."

Holding my tea up and watching the steam rise, I asked, "What about trees? Is there enough of them?"

Cup in hand, Stefon pointed his finger at me. "I have faith in you, Kezel. After the work you did in those woods back in camp, this should be an adventure."

Snuffing my cigarette out on the corner of the wood stove, I stepped over a pile of clothes laying at Stefon's feet and set my cup on the table. "That's what the Army Recruiter said when I signed their contract to stay out of jail... 'It'll be an adventure of a lifetime.' Look where the fuck I am now." I patted Arek's shoulders and gave Katya a sneering smile. "But...I've never had such great friends."

Katya brushed a few strands of hair from her face. "And?"

I grinned, looking at the door. "Hmm."

"What's the problem?" she shot back. "I thought you grew up on the American frontier and knew everything there is to know about making log cabins and tepees." Picking up her cup with two hands, she glanced into it. "With what we see of America on the television, you should be able to build a cabin by yourself in a day or two."

"Cowboys and Indians, hoo...yeah." Taking out my knife, I eyed its edge as I slid my thumb along it. "The Indians still raid our settlements once in awhile." I pointed the blade at her. "In fact I have a hankering to scalp your braids and hang 'em on my belt."

Flipping her long black braids behind her back, she set her cup down. "You touch me and you'll find out what this native does to disrespectful foreigners."

"Damn it, Arek. She's got no sense of humor." I put my knife away and reached for my coat on the floor. "I'm outta here—"

Arek put his foot on it.

I gave a gentle tug trying to pull it free. "Look, whatever you guys want, I'm in."

"Thank you," Arek said, removing his foot. "We'll need to get started right away."

"Draw up the plans, while I go outside. And I mean, I gotta go."

* * *

For the next five days I cut trees down. Stefon followed behind cutting off the limbs, while Arek prepped the ground for the add-on. Tired of swinging the axe, I tried picking up the butt of the tree I had just chopped down. "Damn it, Arek," I yelled at him through the brush as he was measuring one of the other logs.

"What's the matter?"

"It's going take more than the three of us to drag these things out of here."

"Yeah, I've been thinking about that, too."

Stefon could be heard struggling to make his way through the brush towards me. Suddenly his movements went quiet. "Ugh, Oww. How about we talk about this over lunch?"

"What's the matter? The Devil gettin' the better of you with his thorny vines?"

"Never! But my stomach is."

During the meal, we talked of all sorts of ideas on how to move the logs down to the cabin. But each one had a flaw; Lack of time before winter came. Then Stefon came up with, "Why don't we cut the logs shorter and make a five-sided addition."

Arek drew it out on the floor with charcoal. It looked feasible. Then he did the math on the floor too, figuring the biggest log would be light enough for the three of us to handle. Katya walked in the door as Arek finished writing his calculations out. With her hands on her hips, she looked at the floor. Smiling, I tossed her a rag. "We're finished. Now it's your turn."

Focusing on the drawing, Katya sat next to Arek on the bunk. "You think it'll big enough?"

"It should double what we have."

Throwing her arms around his neck, she peeked over his shoulder at me and tossed the rag into my lap as she raved, "Oh thank you, I knew you could."

Arek and I, able to drag most of the shorter cut logs to the house, left Stefon to sort through the limbs in order to find the right ones for the roof. Katya, in anticipation, stayed in the cabin fixing a large dinner to celebrate our effort.

After finishing the meal, Stefon rapped his knuckles on the table. "Tomorrow is the Sabbath and we should not work. The Lord says to rest on his day."

I gave him a crazed look. "Why?"

"Scripture," using his hand, he made a cross in front of himself. "Thou shall not work on the—."

He had barely finished with his sign when I cut him off. Holding up my hand with fingers spread wide, I insisted, "We escaped on a Tuesday, traveled for six days, and arrived here." I fluttered my fingers in a rapid motion to distract him. "Then, we worked five more before you began doing something easy that shouldn't be called work at all. Now..." I smirked, "after one day of doing nothing, you want to declare Friday, a day off, instead of Sunday."

"My friend," Stefon reached over and squeezed my fingers. "I like it when you challenge me about the Lord, but your math is wrong." He let go and leaned his back against the wall. "Tomorrow is Wednesday, not Friday, and the Lord doesn't care what day you choose, as long as you choose one."

I pulled out a smoke, lighting it. "OK. I choose Sunday. The day God chose."

Arek reached up, taking his carving project from the shelf above the table, laughed, "He's got you there, Stefon."

The priest smoothed his beard with his fingers. "You'll be working by yourself."

"Wait a minute," I tried blowing a smoke ring at him. "Isn't this a joint effort. You know, all for one and one for all."

He swatted at the smoke. "We'll take a vote."

Katya's hand shot up. "I vote yes."

Leaning forward, I picked up my cup from the table. "That's not very communist like."

Stefon got to his feet. "Exactly, comrade."

CHAPTER SIX

The next morning, in observance of our, 'day of rest', Katya and Arek went to visit the old woman over the hill. Stefon decided to spend the morning in prayer. And I, laid in my bed on the floor for several hours before deciding to go check on the car, making sure it would still start. I also wanted a piece of mind that everything had been gathered from it.

The thick frost crunching under my feet on the trail, reminded me that winter was still coming. Jumping over the water seep crossing the trail, it occurred to me, *I'm going to have to find something to do. I'll go flippin' nuts stuck in that cabin with her during them long cold nights.*

Looking at the car, I stood listening to the silence all around me as my breath formed a cloud in the air. The loneliness of the mountains seemed to make the shadows around the car darker than normal. Stepping next to the frozen hulk of steel, I rubbed at the frost on one of the windows. "Oh well, I'll have to think of something after we finish the cabin." I pulled fruitlessly on the frozen door. "In the meantime, I'm gunna need something to pry this damn thing open."

* * *

It took ten more days of working dawn to dark, for the three of us to finish the shell of the addition. Leaving many of the cracks between the logs not fully chinked in order to get the roof done. The last of the moss covering had been put in place, when the clouds rapidly rolled in and started snowing heavily while we ate our supper.

Hesitant about sleeping in the new addition for fear the roof might collapse in the middle of the night without being tested, I balked at moving in. Stefon stood in the doorway and prayed a blessing of strength on it. "It's safe now my friend."

Katya quickly seized at the oppertunity. "Arek, he doesn't trust your work. I trust you, and I think we should take the room so I can have privacy. Out here," she waved her arm, "there is none."

Arek nodded in agreement. "What do you think, Kezel?"

"There's an old saying...you want privacy, go to the privy. That's what it's for."

Katya wrinkled her nose at me. "That's lame."

"Fine by me," I shrugged. "It would mean I could sleep closer to the stove. And while putting wood on the fire in the middle of the night, I wouldn't have ta worry about her modesty issues."

Rolling her eyes, she placed her cup on the table. "This isn't some men's club, you know."

I snapped my fingers at her. "Get on the other side of your curtain."

Curling her hand into a fist, she shook it at me. "Watch it, buster."

"You, better be careful," I brushed her off with my hand. "Or I'll get a piece of chalk and draw lines on the floor."

"I'll draw a line with my boot up your—."

Arek got up and put his hand on her shoulders. "He's jerking your chain. Come on, let's go to bed."

"She's lucky she didn't touch me," I snickered as she snatched the blankets from their bunk. "I'd hate to tattle on her to mommy."

"Go to bed," she yelled, as my blankets came flying from behind the curtain.

* * *

Stepping out on the porch the next morning, I looked at the snow as I stretched. There was a snow drift from the addition into the trees beyond the outhouse. Only a small portion of the flat roofed toilet was visible above the snow. Walking away from the cabin towards the trees, I found a spot to relieve myself. Waltzing back into the cabin, I shouted, "Hey everyone, the snow's covered the outhouse."

Katya stepped from behind the curtain. "Go dig it out. I want a path, and space for the door to swing open wide."

"Man-up and do what we do...write in the snow," I shot back.

Arek put his tea down. "Come on, it shouldn't take long while she cooks breakfast."

The wind filled in the dug out path in a matter of a few hours. Around noon, wanting to use the outhouse, Stefon cleared the path again. Then, Arek did it a third time after Katya returned from the outside, whining she had trouble opening the door to get out.

By dark, our pregnant housemate got to use a warm private chamber pot in her room behind the curtain. Mean while, we men were forced to use a bucket on the porch, so much for escaping from the prison lifestyle.

As the storm raged on for several more days blowing snow drifts one way, then another, ice crystals swirling around on the porch, stung any exposed flesh every time I used the bucket. Tired of the painful experiences, I demanded Katya share her warm indoor pot. Quickly she volunteered to stitch some of the unusable clothing together to make a crude curtain around the bucket.

Cabin fever set in on the fifth day of being stuck inside. After breakfast, yelling I was ready to kill her if she made one more snipe, Arek stepped between us trying to ease the tension. "Kezel, you need something to occupy yourself."

"Yeah, like what?"

"How about carving us some more spoons...or maybe forks?"

"Yeah, you're right. Unlike some people, I can't sleep all day." I picked a limb from the wood box. "But, then again," I weighted the limb in my hand, "maybe I should just thump—"

A loud banging on the door cut me short.

Dropping the wood, I grabbed the pistol from its holster hanging on the wall and slammed my back against the wall next to the door.

Arek snatched the rifle from its pegs above the woodstove and knelt, aiming at the door.

Stefon stood in front of the door with his shoulder pressed against it, looking at me.

I cocked the revolver and nodded.

He opened the door a crack and peeked out. Seeing nothing, he opened the door a little further and stuck his head out. Biting my lip and squeezing the pistol harder, my heart pounded in anticipation of the police kicking the door open.

"Welcome!" Stefon bellowed as he stepped aside, flinging the door wide open. "Come in, come in."

A hooded figure with a walking staff and carrying a basket stepped in.

"Well, well. If it isn't Baba Yaga," I snorted while carefully letting the hammer down.

"Kezel!" Katya snapped from behind the curtain. "Quit being disrespectful."

Wiping the sweat from my forehead, I snarled back, "Don't get me goin' woman, I still have the gun in my hand."

The old woman smiled as she held out her basket. Stefon took it, setting it on the table. Brushing the snow off her shawl, she stamped her feet three times before stepping in and closing the door. Bowing to each of us, she made her way towards the stove. With her hands close to its hot surface, the old woman began speaking in a language I wasn't familiar with. It sounded like she was repeating some sort of a chant.

Katya pushed the curtain aside, stepping into the room she bowed to the old woman and joined in the chanting. Together they repeated what sounded like the same words over three times. Smiling as she finished, our guest took her fur-lined parka off and threw it over the back of a chair.

Rubbing her palms together, she gently placed a weathered hand on Katya's extended belly. With the cracks on the old woman's face, it was hard to see her grin as she spoke, "All is well. I was afraid the spirits that Vlad allows in this cabin might have frighten the child and cause complications."

Stefon stopped pawing through the basket and gave the old woman a stern look. "My dear woman, I assure you that I have asked for Christ's blessings on this humble house."

The old woman continued to knead Katya's belly with her fingertips, ignoring his comment. After a few more minutes of prodding, the old woman started chanting something new.

Katya, looking at me, pointed to the tea kettle. "It's empty. Our guest is thirsty."

Defiant, I stared back and growled, "Baba Yaga."

Katya squinted. "Pleeease."

Returning the revolver to its holster on the wall, then roughly brushing past her to get to the kettle. "Next, I suppose, you're gunna ask me to crawl in the oven."

She snapped her fingers. "Kezel, you're being disrespectful."

I grabbed my coat from its peg by the door and shoved my arm through a sleeve. "Damn, you sound just like a witch I know." Before she could say anything, I stepped out and slammed the door.

By the time I returned with the kettle, Stefon had found the fruit-filled pastries in the basket. Pulling one apart and placing the little morsel in his mouth, he acted like he had never tasted anything so sweet.

Arek and Katya, sitting next to the old woman, rubbed her hands while all three pairs of eyes followed me across the room. I set the kettle on the stove and stared out the small window behind it. "Why do I feel like I'm in a flippin' fairy tale?" My foot bumped the empty water pail next to the stove. "Which one could it be, Cinderella?" Snatching the bucket, I headed for the door. "Uhmmm. Maybe Hansel and Gretel?" Jerking the door open and standing there letting the wind blow in, I waited for Katya to say something. All I got was silence. Stepping out, I threw another jab, "Nah, can't be Sleeping Beauty."

Packing the wooden pail full of snow from a drift in the yard, I left it on the porch steps before heading to check on the outhouse. With the privy still half-buried in a drift, I worked my way to the closest tree and wrote my name in the snow at its base before going back into the house.

Carrying the bucket past our guest, she looked up at me, grinning, "Ahh, the young weasel returns to steal a tasty morsel from my house."

I winked at her. "Careful, babushka, I may have lived among the urki, but that doesn't mean I am one." Setting the bucket in its place next to the stove, I turned to her and grinned, "Besides, gypsies are smarter than fuckin' Russians."

Katya rose, stepping toward me with her nostrils flaring and clenched fists. The old woman stayed her with a hand on her arm. "Don't worry child. My skin has become thick over the years. I don't mind."

Stefon spoke up, entering the melee. "My dear woman, these are such exquisite pastries."

Opening my mouth and raising my hand in an effort to emphasize my comment, Stefon cut me off, "You came all this way with such wonderful pastries."

I glared at him. "Didn't you Poles learn a culinary damn thing from the Germans?"

"On the contrary, my friend," he smiled. "It was the Polish who taught the Germans how to make apple-strudel."

The old woman froze, wide-eyed. Staring at Stefon for several minutes, she carefully rose from her chair. Eyeing him from one angle, and then another, much like a bird in the grass looking for worms, she began to walk around his chair. When she finished her circle, she dropped to her knees in front of him and cradled his hands in hers. Kissing the backs of his, she started babbling in her native tongue.

Stefon stared at Katya with a puzzled look on his face.

Katya's face paled. "I think...she's apologizing...umm...to the one who saved her as a child?" She glanced at Stefon, then at Arek. "I don't...she's speaking in the tongue of the elders. It's an old dialect that few understand."

In all the time knowing Stefon, he never failed at his ability to quickly come to grips with people's actions. Expecting this to be a first, I watched, intrigued with how he was going to fumble through it.

Waiting for the old woman to pause in her rambling, he brought her hands up to his lips and kissed her fingers. Then lifting her hands, encouraging her to stand, he asked, "Please, you are such a wonderful storyteller. Will you share the story with our friends?"

The old woman bowed her head. "As you wish."

She positioned her chair to face Katya and Arek. Not wanting to be left out, I sat on the floor next to them and leaned against the wall. Stefon picked up his chair, placing it next to me. The old woman began by making the sign of the crucifixion while speaking in Russian this time. "I was but a small child when the revolution came to the Amur region. Many Czech and Polish soldiers had come to protect the railroad from the Bolsheviks. The European warriors were gallant, fearless fighters."

The old woman became very animated with her hands in conveying the elements of her story. "My father sold them firewood, and vegetables from our garden. While my mother mended their garments. In exchange, the soldiers protected us from the cruelty of the Red Army..."

Sliding forward in her chair, she continued, "It happened one day, while I was riding on the pile of wood in my father's wagon. As we crossed the bridge over a small river just outside of the camp's main gate, a wheel came off father's wagon. I tumbled right into the icy water. Mother's screams caught the attention of a sentry at the gate. The young, dark-haired guard throwing down his rifle and pack, jumped into the swift flowing river to save me.

Mother and father, neither of whom knew how to swim, could not express their gratitude enough to the young man for rescuing me...their only child. The next day my father went to the fort with presents for the young man, but he wasn't there. He had gone to Smirna that morning to fight the Red Army and was not seen again."

The old woman rose from her chair and gave Stefon a hug. "Until now. He has returned so I may pay my debt."

Stefon stammered," I...I...I..."

"Babushka," I piped up, "tell us more about this man who saved you."

"Later. I have to prepare a feast in his honor." Smiling, she placed her hand on top of my head. "Fetch me a pail of water, young weasel."

"It's Kezel," I growled.

"Either way, they sound the same." Turning away, she asked, "Would you like to eat?"

"Yes, ma'am."

"Then be off, young man."

That evening, the old woman fixed the best meal I had in years. Complemented with stories of her childhood, and many about Katya's family. As the evening wore on, it was decided that Stefon would go live with the old woman. In doing so, it would give her a chance to repay her debt, and also provide her with companionship during the long winter.

Not to mention, giving me more room in the cabin.

CHAPTER SEVEN

With Stefon gone, our pregnant room-mate quickly decided to make the crowded two-room cabin much like an organized vacation home. She had Arek rip out Stefon's bunk, and me, drag the table over to where the bunk was. Then the shelving above where the table had been, needed to come down before moving my bed closer to the door.

Finishing her 'to do list', Arek and I decided to check on the car. But before we could get out the door, Katya announced she didn't like how it looked and demanded everything be put back in its original spot before we leave.

When we returned from checking on the car, she made it plain she wanted a different arrangement. Her rearranging merry-go-round had me sneaking outside constantly for a smoke break. Arek somehow managed to keep his sanity through the fifth re-arrangement, until I came back in and lost it when Katya shoved an empty water bucket against my chest snapping, "Fill it."

Dropping the hammer in my hand on the floor next to her feet, I ran my tongue around my teeth several times as I stared at her. She pushed the pail against my chest again. "That's it, Arek. I'm outta here. I'm flat-ass tired of her bull shit." Snatching my coat off my bunk, I headed for the door. "I'm going for a walk."

Outside on the porch, the intense sunlight from the clear blue sky reflecting off the snow, burned my eyes. I tried squinting, it wasn't enough, I had to cover my eyes with my hand. In my blindness, I heard the door open and could tell it was Arek stepping out.

"You're not gunna change my mind."

"I don't plan to. Here, you'll need this."

I held my hand out behind my back expecting him to give me the pistol. Instead, he placed the handle of the pail in my hand. Gritting my teeth and shaking my head, I brought the bucket around in front of me.

Lying in the bottom was a pair of the snow goggles he had carved while in the gulag.

"Figured you'll need those," he said, stepping along side me and slipping on a pair.

Tossing the bucket into the snow, I slipped the wooden visor over my eyes. It was like looking through a knot hole. The narrow slits restricted sight so immensely, I could only see my hands if I held them out at arms length. "Wow, this is gunna be fun."

Arek took one step forward, "Which way you plan on going?"

Standing at the top of the stairs looking towards the outhouse, I pointed, "There's a track just beyond the privy, taking off from the main trail." Holding my foot out, I waved it around guessing where the step down should be, "It goes towards what looks like a shel—"

Missing the step and landing in a heap in the snow, I raised my arm, laughing, "I'm gunna head that way, if I can find the bucket."

"It's a little to your left."

Rolling over, my hand brushed against it as I got to my knees. "Ah there it is."

"Mind if I go with you?" he asked stepping off the porch.

"Are you sure you want to leave her by herself?"

"Yeah, she'll be OK."

We made our way over to the wood pile. I pulled the small hand axe from the chopping block. "I don't mind at all. In fact..." I shoved its handle under my belt, "I'd be happy to have you along. I just thought you'd want to stay with her."

"Yeah, that's what I thought too, at first. But her fluffing the nest, is driving me nuts. Dang—" he stumbled, slipping in the snow. "Besides, I think we need to talk about setting up some sort of trap line."

I ducked under a limb hanging across the path and laughed to myself, *We're barely into winter and he's already looking for a reason to escape from the witch.* Standing up on the other side, I rose into the tangled mess of another limb. "Damn it." Waving my arms around in an effort to get free, "Didn't I say...you got a tiger on your hands? And now she's about ready to bite your head—" I my hat fell off.

"I can handle her, it's the sitting around with nothing to do. I can't do that."

"So what do you propose?" Reaching down to pick up my hat, I slipped and fell. "Oww! You know I'm leaving in the spring. Regardless."

"I know. That's why I want you to teach me how to trap. It may become our only source of income once all the cash and jewelry are gone."

"You're gunna need—" Standing up snow fell off my hat and down my back. "*Eeaahhh!* Damn that's cold." Looking at him, I opened my coat, shaking it out. "You're gunna need to know more than what little I can teach you."

Arek slipped, falling down in the same spot where I had. "*Umphf,* damn it. I'm not used to walking in this deep of snow."

The snow still trapped inside my coat started to melt. Taking my coat off to shake it out, my goggles fell to the ground. "Hey, it's shaded enough in the trees we don't...wait a minute, didn't Vasiy say he was gunna get you some working papers?"

Standing up, Arek brushed himself off and put his visor in his pocket. "They don't guarantee work. They just say that you can work."

The trail we were following disappeared under the snow at the top of the ridge. Standing on the highest point, we could see down the slope of the other side into a wooded ravine. There in the bottom, about a hundred meters away, was a ribbon of flowing water that hadn't completely froze yet. From our position, I searched for a good way to get down to the water and fill the bucket. A movement next to the stream caught my attention. "A deer! Damn it, why didn't I bring the rif—."

The loud explosion, an arm's length from my head, knocked me to my knees. Through the pain of it all, I could barely hear Arek yelling,

"I got him! I got him," as he raced down the hill. Grabbing handfuls of snow and holding them to my head in an effort to numb the throbbing in my ears. Arek, in his excitement, half-ran, half-slide down to the bottom. Staying on my knees, I held my breathe watching him as he ran towards the wounded animal, *Wait for it...wait for it...waaait.*

Stopping a few meters from the struggling animal, Arek stood still, staring at it.

"Yep, that's what I thought. Never shot one before." Getting to my feet, I headed down the hill.

When I approached Arek, I could see the bullet had shattered the deer's spine, making its back legs useless. The deer was crying a gut wrenching wail as it fought to stand. The sight and sound of it's plight had Arek obviously shaken. I glanced over at him. "You gunna finish the job?"

His face pale as the snow, asked, "How?"

Grabbing the rifle from his hands, I jacked another round into the chamber. "First you step behind the animal, thrust the end of the barrel against the back of its head...and pull the trigger."

The deer dropped to the ground lifeless as the sound of the gunshot echoed in the valley. Tossing the rifle to Arek, I pulled out my knife and dug my knee into the animal's shoulder. Reaching around its neck, I slit its throat. Watching the snow turn red, I stepped away from the deer and patted Arek on the shoulder. "Just like that."

"I...I've never done anything like this back home." Arek looked away. "I've...never taken a life before."

"Shit, you damn near took mine with that shot." I walked over to where I had dropped the bucket. Holding out the pail, I offered, "Go get some water and I'll get started on the deer."

Taking a deep breath, then slowly letting it out, Arek shook his head. "No, I need to learn. I'll do the deer, you get the water."

"Why the hell am I always stuck with the water?"

We stood there for a moment in silence staring at the deer. I waited for Arek to move. Wiping his nose on his sleeve, he finally reached for his knife. I pressed the axe handle against his arm to stop him. "How about you cut a pole long enough to tie the thing on, and we'll carry it home. That way Katya can clean it."

Grinning, he raised his eyebrows. "Yeah, we most likely wouldn't do it right by her."

It was a battle trying to carry anything and climb up the hill. After an hour long half-ass endeavor to get to the top, the sun had dropped behind the trees enough to make us move faster. We got the deer, and half a bucket of water, to the cabin just at dark.

Katya, stepping from the outhouse as Arek and I reached the porch, yelled at us, "I just cleaned that house and you two aren't taking anything inside."

Arek dropped his end of the pole. "Come see what I shot."

Choosing her steps carefully in the snow till she got next to Arek, her face lit up. She could hardly contain herself as she danced around in the snow. "Hang it up on the porch. I'll get a knife," she yelled, racing into the cabin.

I hadn't finished tying the rope around its head before she was back out with an eight inch blade and started slicing the belly open. "Whoa, whoa, wait till we get this thing up, will you?"

"Hurry up then. I'm hungry."

"We'll get it up in a second, just hold your horses." I wrapped my arms around the animal's chest and lifted. "OK Arek, pull!"

The back feet of the deer had barely left the porch floor when she jumped forward and snapped, "That's good."

Holding the carcass still while Arek tied the rope around the porch railing, I asked her, "You want me to show you how to—"

Elbowing me out of the way, Katya opened up an animal's belly faster than I'd ever seen done before. "O...K. I guess you don't—"

As the organs oozed out, she pointed her knife at me, "Unless you want to lose some fingers, you better go find a couple of buckets and stay out of my way."

"Yes, ma'am." Fetching two buckets from the woodshed, I dropped them at her feet and stood back watching her fill one with the heart, liver, and kidneys. The other with the intestines, lungs, and stomach. With the body cavity empty, she sliced out the tender loins and tossed them in with the heart.

Bloody up to her elbows, Katya took a step back from her work and bowed to Arek. "You have provided well for us, husband." Picking up the pail with the tender loins, she brushed past me, "Some day, you may become a great hunter like him."

"Yeah, some day I might."

At the door she paused, "Supper will be ready soon, I expect you'll be done by then."

Shaking my head, I glanced over at Arek, "Damn, who's gunna kill who first." Taking the knife out that Katya had stabbed into the animals shoulder, I pulled on a front leg. "This is how I learned to skin the damn things."

In the process of pulling the hide off, I accidentally knocked the bucket full of guts down the stairs. Arek raised his eyebrows, "Should we..."

"Leave it, I don't eat that stuff. Besides, once it's frozen, it'll be easier to clean up."

After pulling the hide free, I laid it out on the snow at the bottom of the steps, then helped Arek carry the carcass inside to cut up.

Katya gave us one of her looks, "What are you doing?"

I turned around, looking at her. "Bringing it in to cut up."

"Take it back outside. Supper is ready."

Arek started to put his end of the carcass down, "OK, we'll do—"

"NOW."

Carrying our winter supply of meat out the door and knowing it could be tomorrow before anything was done with it, I muttered, "Let's just get it up as high as we can. I got a feeling its gunna be here all night."

During supper, Katya asked Arek to tell her how he had shot the deer. When he came to the end, she looked at him, "Wait, how did you see it down there?"

When he repeated that part, there was a slight embellishment to the story.

Smiling, Katya looked at me and asked, "Now, who saw the deer first?"

I pointed to Arek.

Katya patted his arm. "That's what I thought. My man the mighty hunter."

With my belly stretched to its limit, I pushed back from the table and lit a cigarette. "Wow! Finally, something we both agree on. Now, oh mighty hunter, where we going to put the meat so it won't spoil?"

Arek snapped his fingers. "Hold that thought. We forgot something."

Reaching up on the shelf above his head, he brought down a bottle of vodka and poured a drink for everyone, then returned the bottle to its spot on the shelf.

Katya raised her glass. "To Arek, the mighty hunter."

I tapped her glass with mine. "And may he be successful again and again. Without making me deaf."

She snorted.

Before she could speak, I cheered, "To Arek," and drained my cup. I winced at the burning in my throat and hammered the table with the cup. "Uggh. Whoa, damn! Haven't felt that in awhile." Gasping for air, I glanced around the cabin blinking, trying to clear the moisture from my eyes. "Yeah...looks like we need more water to finish cleaning the meat. I'll get some snow while I'm outside doing my thing."

Leaning over, I sluggishly picked up the pail. Upright and on my feet, I slowly shuffled towards the door. The thought of all that work so soon after supper didn't sound as appealing as my bunk. "Tomorrow, maybe." I exhaled loudly and started singing, "To-mar-row...to-mar-row is only..." Pulling the door open, I asked, "Hey, Arek, what do think of letting it hang on the por—"

Seeing light reflecting off a pair of cold yellow eyes belonging to a wolf at the bottom of the steps. I froze, staring at it. The wolf, its mouth full of the spilled deer guts, didn't move either as it stared back at me.

"I don't see why not, when you get...what's the matter?"

"Get the rifle," I whispered, not about to take my eyes off the beast.

The wolf, standing his ground, growled louder.

"Arrrek... Get your ass over here with that damn rifle?"

"I'm right behind you, Kezel. What's the—"

Hearing the click of the safety as he pushed it off, I reached behind me feeling around for him. "Don't pull the trigger yet. Make sure there's a round in the chamber, first."

The bolt clacked as he opened it. "There's one," he said sliding it closed.

The wolf put one foot on the bottom stair and growled louder.

"When I step out of the way, shoot. OK?"

"Yes."

"Ready...no—"

Arek pulled the trigger before I moved. The muzzle blast knocked me into the door, slamming it shut. Laying on the floor with my hands over my ears, I screamed, "What the fuck."

Looking at me with a dumb look on his face, Arek scrunched up his shoulders. "Sorry." "Fucking sorry doesn't help." I took a swipe at his legs with my foot. "You were suppose to wait for me to get out of the way."

Upright with my back against the door, I could see Katya jumping up and down yelling, "My man, the mighty hunter."

Kneeling beside me, Arek laid the rifle on the floor and tried to console me. "I'm sorry, I didn't want to... I mean, I didn't mean to..."

Taking my hands away from my ears, all I could hear was Katya's screeching, "Did you get him? Did you get him?"

I couldn't tell what hurt worse, the ringing in my ears or her screaming. "Shut the fuck up," I yelled, squeezing my head. The bouncing floor stopped moving. Looking over at her, she stood there with her hands on her hips and a look of disgust on her face. I glared back, "You got a fuckin' problem?"

"You better watch your mouth. Or you're gunna have a problem."

"Fuck you, you ain't my mother." Crawling up the door, I leaned against it. "Get me the damn pistol, woman. Then we'll find out if he got it or not."

I patted Arek on the shoulder as he tried to help me step away from the door. "You think you hit the damn thing?"

"I'm pretty sure."

"What? I can't hear you."

He leaned the rifle against the wall and raised his voice. "I was aiming for its shoulder, and I thought I saw him go down."

"Good, we're gunna do it right this time." I reached out to take the pistol from Katya as she stepped next to Arek.

Defiantly, she shoved me out of the way and flung the door open. The wolf lay at the bottom of the steps, dead. She let out a whoop. "Yes, I knew—"

Suddenly a second creature leaped from the shadows, running across the porch. Without hesitation Katya raised the revolver and pulled the trigger, hitting the second wolf in the left eye. It tumbled down the stairs and laid still on top of its mate.

Standing in the doorway with my mouth open, Arek pressed past me and gave her a hug. "She was luc...key," I muttered.

Grasping hold of the bucket on the floor and stepping out onto the porch, I poked Arek shoulder next to Katya's hand. "I think maybe she should be the one to teach you how to hunt and trap."

Katya let go of him and huffed, "You're damn right I should." She turned, going into the cabin and brought out a lantern. "Women..." she held it out towards me, "end up teaching men everything they know anyway."

Arek took the light from her. "Thank you, we'll take it from here." Katya stood with her arms folded looking at him. "That's OK, we'll take care of them." She didn't move. Arek put his hand on her shoulder. "It's cold out here, you should go back inside for the baby's sake."

She nodded while rubbing her arms, then stepped in closing the door.

Leaning close to me after the door latched, I could see Arek had lost his usual smile. "Hunting's not the issue...in another month or two she's going to...you know. And I'm going to need you're help."

Stepping back away from him, I held up my hand. "What? You think I've delivered babies, too?"

His face paled, taking on a serious look. "I've never done it before. I'm going to...to need some kind of support."

The frantic look on his face was enough to make me laugh. The more I laughed, the more flustered he got. "You're not helping," he snapped.

"OK. OK." I tried putting on a serious look. "You're going to need more than my support. Especially...if...she gets her hands on that pistol...during labor." I burst out laughing again.

"Kezel, give me a break, this my first child."

Katya came out holding two sharpened knives. Glancing at Arek as I took the knives from her, "Well, you're one ahead of me." Handing him one, I took a step toward the closest wolf. "When that day happens, I'll go get Stefon. And, eh, maybe the old babushka. But for now, we need to get those pelts off them critters before Katya skins us."

* * *

The snow seemed to never melt. It just got deeper. When we laid out our first trap line, neither one of us knew how to walk in the deep snow. Katya had to teach us to improvise, using fir boughs for snowshoes. As the weeks progressed, I kept adding traps. It didn't take long and walking the line grew from a four hour round trip hike, to an all day ordeal.

The first time the line kept me away from the cabin for six hours, Arek cornered me on the porch as I was skinning the day's catch. "What do you think about adding another trap line in the old woman's valley?"

"Why? This one keeps me busy enough."

"Yes, so I've noticed. But I'm thinking it would be a good way to check in on Stefon."

"Sure." I draped the rabbit pelt in my hands over the porch railing. "I think I could handle more traps. And, that would make it easier for me to take them some of the meat."

"No, no, I can do it. You have enough on your plate."

"Ahhh, I see. You need to get away from...her." I winked.

Looking down at the porch floor, Arek scuffed at a piece of frozen mud with his toe. "Her attitude is growing bigger than her belly. Whenever I bring a project into the cabin and set it down, she screams at me, 'don't you drag that dirty thing in here,' then pushes me outside." He began stroking the rabbit's fur. "I need some space."

I knew what he was saying. In order to handle her attitude, I started thinking of her as an older sister, with the idea that I could be as snotty to her as I wanted, and she'd have to live with it. Seeing the glazed look on Arek's face while he stroked the fur, I could hear the familiar words, *What more do you need when you're with people you think of as family,* from one of Tomas' arguments.

Tomas was right, living in Siberia had become my life. I have two hots and a cot; and two good friends. Along with a pregnant, nagging sister, and a babushka. Reaching over and patting his shoulder, I nodded. "Sure thing my friend. I'd be happy to share this wide outdoors with you. That line 'ill be all yours."

Turning back to my work, I knew deep down inside, I still had a craving to escape. And it wasn't because of her.

* * *

The week after establishing the new trap line, me and Arek, decided to pay Stefon and the old woman a visit. Stefon was so excited to see us walk in the door, he struggled to hang onto his tea cup. "My friends, my friends, I am so glad to see you. I have great news."

Giving Stefon a customary hug, Arek laughed asking, "You finally learned to cook?"

"Better, my friend." He put an arm around Babushka's shoulders. "Through her contacts with other tribal members, they have found me a small parish in a village just outside the city of Lidoga. Their elderly priest has become terminally ill and they need someone to take his place before the local committee decides to shutter the church."

As we sat drinking tea, Arek made the mistake of asking the old woman what the church was like. For the next ten minutes, she apologized continually to Stefon while carrying on that the church had no golden dome, no gold chalices or icons, not many parishioners, but it that would still be perfect for him.

Stefon put his hand on hers. "You've done more than enough to repay your debt, my dear woman."

"No," Babushka shook her head. "I won't hear of it. I can never repay you enough."

Glancing at Arek, I rolled my eyes. "Here we go again."

The two of them carried on with their back and forth prattle of, 'no I haven't, yes you have.' About the fifth time around the mulberry bush,

I leaned over to Arek. "I'll see you back at the cabin." Rising to my feet, I bumped Stefon's shoulder with my elbow. "When you leaving?"

"Three days from now,Friday."

"I have hides to attend to, I'll see you then." Bowing to Babushka, I took her hand, "Thank you for the tea."

Arek jumped to his feet, grabbing her hand after I let go. "Uhm, I have to go too. We've set up a second trapline for me. And I need to learn how to work it."

* * *

When it was time for Stefon to leave at the end of the week, I convinced Arek not to say anything to Katya about going over to Babushka's. We left her in the cabin re-arraigning things as normal. Stopping at the woodshed and grabbing our packs, Arek hoisted his and swung it behind his back. "I still don't think it was a good idea not to tell her."

"Are you kidding?" I squawked while shoving Stefon's share of Zarkhov's trunk treasure in my coat pocket. Then with a bit of sarcasm, I went off on a tirade. "If you did, she'd want to go. Then we'd have to wait over an hour for her to make up her mind on which pair of pants to wear. Once we got on the trail, then she'd bitch about the long walk. And then, at Babushka's she'd be...Arek, get me this, Arek...get me that—"

"You're full of it, she wouldn't do that."

Hitting a snow burdened branch over hanging the trail with my walking stick, I paused letting the snow fall before glancing back at Arek. "You wouldn't get any time with Stefon."

No, she would let me—"

"She'd be pulling on your leash."

"Nev...hmmm," he sucked in a deep breath, "maybe...OK, I get your point."

Arriving at Babushka's to the scent of fresh made fruit pastries, and finding she had put them in a box for Stefon. I was about to lament about it, when I noticed she had put a few on the table, along with a pot of strong sweet tea. She motioned for us to gather around and sit.

By the time the teapot was empty, their prattle once more had me climbing the walls. I excused myself from the table with the pretense of using the outhouse. Arek apparently didn't get my hint and continued to smile, listening the old woman. When I opened the door, he looked over in my direction. Grabbing Stefon's sleeve, he tugged on it. "Come on. Vasiy is waiting."

Looking up at them from the porch step where I sat smoking a cigarette, I waited for the door to be closed before opening my mouth. "It's about time. Let's hope Vasiy will still be there."

The path from her house to the traveled road, was a short gentle one compared to ours.

When it was obvious we were out of earshot from the cabin, Stefon finally spoke up. "Thank you Arek."

"For what?"

"For helping to get me away from her."

"You gotta be kidding," I laughed. "You must have gained twenty pounds living there."

"My friend, you don't know how hard it is to leave her cooking. She could make the root of a tree taste like pastry." He sighed. "And dried grass, as exquisite as frytki."

"What's that?" I asked.

"I believe the Germans call them, Pommes frites."

Arek put his arm around Stefan's shoulder and shook him. "I'm going to miss you, my friend. Especially your cuisine revelations."

Stepping out of the trees into a large sloping meadow, the road came into view. A small cloud of black smoke drifted from the truck's exhaust stack as it sat waiting. At the sight of the truck our merriment stopped and a sobering silence took over. Halfway across the meadow,

Stefon bumped my arm. "Something is bothering you, Kezel. What is it?"

"I...I owe you a lot. You helped me keep going in those first dark days." My face flushed. "Shit, I'm beginning to sound like the old woman." I mimicked her words, "I haven't done enough for you."

"Please," Stefon crossed himself and raised his eyes to the sky, "don't start with that. It is I, who owes you." Arek shook his head in affirmation to Stefon's words. "If God hadn't placed you in a position of the godfather's good grace, we would have been thrown into the mines."

Stefon chimed in, "And most likely dead by now."

Smiling, I put an arm around the priest. "Still trying to convert me, aren't you. It's not working, my friend."

As we approached the truck, Vasiy climbed out and set an apple crate full of groceries on the ground. He held out an envelope to Stefon. "Your papers."

Stefon, taking the envelope, shoved the documents into his pocket and pumped Vasiy's hand. "Thank you, my friend."

Vasiy looked over at Arek. "How are things with Little Tiger?"

Arek smiled. "Great. She's doing great." He raised his eyebrows while rubbing his hands together. "She's definitely got quite a spirit."

Hissing, I bit my tongue and coughed. Not one for goodbyes, I grabbed Stefon's hand and shook it, "Till we meet again, my friend." Turning, I hoisted the crate on my shoulder and began the walk home.

CHAPTER EIGHT

Winter's darkness began to wane in the middle of Katya's ninth month of pregnancy. I looked for any reason to escape, leaving Arek to deal with her. Especially when she got into one of her 'moods'.

Sitting on the edge of my bunk, scratching my unshaven face and debating on whether to light a cigarette, or put the kettle on for tea. Arek threw the curtain aside and headed for the stove. "I'm sorry, we just can't."

Katya followed right behind him. "But why?"

He filled the kettle with water, then stood there staring into the empty pail. "We have no glass. That's why."

"For what?" I asked.

Arek looked at me with an exasperated look. "She wants a window...I can't just cut a hole in the wall."

Katya slumped into her chair. "But it's dark in there."

Taking that as my cue, I jumped up from my bunk, grabbing my shoes, and headed for the door. "Sorry, can't help ya there, gotta check the traps. See you later."

"I'll go with you." Arek jerked his coat off its hook.

"Arek, where you going?" she whined. "I need you here to rub my back."

I hopped around on the porch putting my shoes on, while Arek, stood in the doorway putting his coat on. "We're out of that lotion you like. I'll go over to Babushka's and get some more. I'll be back."

"Have Ke—"

Arek closed the door before she could finish. "That woman is driving me nuts," he whispered as he buttoned up his coat.

Babushka's house, now became more of a hideout from Katya, for the both of us, rather than from the authorities. The old woman's grandmotherly advice was what Arek claimed he needed and not an escape from dealing with Katya's demanding mood swings. The old

71

woman's advice always came in the form of a story. I craved the entertainment, as it provided an escape from the silence of winter.

On several occasions after Stefon left, I dropped by to leave her a rabbit, only to find a few of the elders from her clan visiting. Occasionally, some brought their grandchildren with them and they would cluster in the front room of her house where she told the children ancestral stories or would do some ancient ritual in their native tongue.

Stefon never talked about these visitations, but knowing it now, would explain why I often met him along the trail with a long list in his hands and a basket hooked over an arm. When asked what he was doing, his response was always, "She said she wanted to make a special meal for me today, and that she was out of these items. It will take me hours to find everything on this list, but, mmm, it's worth every minute."

Showing up a fourth time with rabbits in my hands as she finished giving lessons, Babuska looked at me, "Well young man, do you expect the rabbits to undress themselves?"

"No, ma'am. It's just that they're fresh out of the traps and I find your stories more entertaining than Katya's barking."

"Patience, young man." Picking up a piece of wood, she placed it on the fire in the stove. "It won't be long now and things will change."

"Yeah, that's what Arek keeps saying, too." Placing the rabbits in the sink, I paused and looked at her. "I've been wondering...why do you do the lessons here instead of at the schoolhouse?"

She did a faux spitting on the floor. "We are forbidden to speak our language. And to teach the old ways, is a crime."

"So why doesn't your clan take over the school and change the rules?"

"My, my, child...haven't you learned yet?" She handed me one of the rattles she had in her hand. "Now that the children have left, I have room for you in the front row."

"No thanks," I handed it back. "I gotta check the last of my traps. Maybe another time."

Walking the trail towards home I had a loud discussion with myself. "I'm goin' to have to make it a point, that if I'm going to stop by her place, I have to run the trapline first. Then I could show up after the children had left, and that way nothing would be left in a trap overnight . Then, maybe, I could get her to talk about the different cultures within the Amur valley. Ahh, why? I ain't gunna be here long. But, then again...knowing why the Evenki and Nevank hate each other. Or why the ruling Soviets have an issue with the Han Chinese... Ah, the info may come useful in getting out of here.

* * *

Showing up at the cabin late three nights in a row, Arek cornered me on the porch. "Kezel, are you having a problem with the traps?"

I shrugged as I pulled out a cigarette. "I'm gathering information for my escape."

"You're really not going to go through with that, are you?"

"Why not? You have a family. Stefon has his church. Me...I have nothing, not even an identity."

"Come on, Kezel. Give it time. Once you have your papers—"

Lighting the cigarette, I lifted an eyebrow, "Once I get those papers my friend, I'm outta here. You're welcome to tag along if you wish."

Arek waved his hand towards Katya inside the cabin. "And leave her before my child is born? No."

Avoiding eye contact with him, I laid my hand on his shoulder. "Look...Arek, you've been a brother to me through thick and thin." Swallowing and trying hard not to choke as images of Masha and Tomas fleeted through my thoughts, I stammered, "I...I...I can't ever forget you, and Stefon. But the truth is...I don't fit in."

He nodded. "I don't agree...but I understand."

Smiling at him with the cigarette stuck in the corner of my mouth, I patted him on the arm. "Now if you don't mind, I have work to do."

The next morning, forgetting my own advice and skipping the trapline, I went straight over to Babushka's in order to ask her about the Japanese invasion of World War Two. And why Mongolians speak Russian instead of Chinese.

Looking at me with curiosity, she asked, "Why do you want to know about that?"

"Well..." Not wanting to tell her the real reason, I offered, "Let's just say, if I'm goin' to live around here, I need to know its history."

"My, my, child. That could take a whole pot of tea to answer, and I'm out of wood. Would you mind?"

Two hours of chopping wood and another hour to get my answers, taught me a hard lesson for not checking the traps first. In all my time trapping, the first time I catch the most valuable sought after animal; an ermine, I caught two. And both were damaged by other critters from being left to long in the traps.

Frustrated with Katya's bitching while trying to salvage the furs, along with anger at my desires to listen to Babuska's stories. I decided it was time to go find the river and plan my way out of here.

The next morning while packing some food, Arek came into the room. "You're packing more than usual, what's up?"

"You mind running my line today? I'm gunna look for a new place to put the traps."

"No, I don't mind." He poured himself a cup of tea. "How long you planning on being gone?"

Taking the rifle off its hooks, I checked how many rounds were in it. "Not long. I'm going towards the valley between here and the river. Gunna do some scouting for fresh signs."

"You'll be back tonight, yes? You know, in case..."

Collecting my pack, I glanced at him and grinned, "Sure thing, it can't be that far."

* * *

I figured wrong, the sun set with me still deep in the woods, and the river was farther away than anticipated. Left with no choice but to search for shelter, I found a rocky outcropping with which I could keep my back against and build a roaring fire for safe measures against the night.

Waking up cold and stiff the next morning as the sunlight filtered through the trees, I rolled onto my knees beside the pile of ashes. Using the hemlock boughs I slept on, I tried rekindling the fire. Stiff from being cold, my fingers found the small twigs to much of a challenge to break. "OK, sister fire, just cause Katya's not—" I breathed on my numb hands, "...come on fingers, bend damn it. Phiff...oh man, come on. Ahh, damn it...if that's the way you want it." I threw all the branches onto the ash pile. "If you start, you start. In the mean time, I'm going up the hill and gunna thaw out in the sun."

Leaving my gear at the bottom and climbing up between the boulders of the twenty-plus meters of broken rock outcropping, I scampered along its ledge to the highest point where it was high enough to get a view over the surrounding trees. Turning to the right, then left, the only thing that could be seen was low lying forested mountains. "Damn...nothing. I wonder if I'm heading in the wrong direction." Pulling out a cigarette and lighting it, I sat down on the rock, soaking up the warmth of the sun. "If only I had... Nahh, with all this glare off the snow, I doubt binoculars would help much."

I caught a whiff of wood smoke drifting in the gentle breeze. Glancing around with my fingers shading my eyes, I looked for a tell tale column of smoke. That's when I realized I had also left the rifle down below alongside my snow goggles. "Ah, damn it. How could I be so stupid as to leave everything down there."

Sliding off the boulder and peeking over the ledge, I saw the branches I had thrown on the ash pile ignited. Scrambling back down,

I set my tin cup full of snow beside the flame and while the snow was melting, cut more branches for a new pair of snowshoes.

Squatting next to the fire while munching on a breakfast of bread and tea, I looked at the cliff I had climbed up and down. "Wait a minute, there's no way I can climb to the top with my pack, a rifle and snowshoes, all strapped to my back. Damn it. That means I'll have ta' leave something here. Or take the flippin' long way around." Standing up, I spit some ice from my mustache into the fire. "As usual, Murphy's here to slow me down."

Fastening the new snowshoes on my feet, I hoisted my pack and hiked along the base of the rock's face searching for that way up. About three hundred meters away, I found a steep slope between rocky outcroppings and climbed in switchback fashion to the top of the hill.

No longer in the shadows of the forest, I was forced to put on the goggles. The view of the horizon took on a new look compared to earlier in the morning. The hills seemed to have shrunk, and a river valley looked to be snaking its way through the mountains in an East by North-East direction. Confident that it was the Amur, I headed in that way.

Coming to a craggy knoll covered with leafless birch trees after hours of hiking, I climbed on top of a boulder to get a better view. Finally, I saw the river itself. Bank to bank, shimmering in the sunlight. It still had to be at least fifteen to twenty kilometers away as the crow flies. But even at that distance it was immense. I stood watching several tiny spots on the water. At first it looked like they were islands. The longer I watched, their slow movements convinced me they had to be barges, gracefully flowing down the river in a line and disappearing around the bend.

When the last one was out of sight, the thought of using the river for my next leg to escape, gave me goosebumps. "Hmm, doggies. In the warmth of the spring thaw, I could ride a log raft tied to one of them barges down to the coast. Then from there... north to the Bering Straights, along the ice pack... on to Alaska."

A cold breeze brushed at the hair in my face, stirring me from my Huck Finn daydream. Glancing up at the sun, it was on a fast descent towards the horizon. "Fuck, I'll never make it back before dark."

Looking around the knoll I was on, it was covered with broken trees. The leafless snags offered nothing for protection against the wind. Hoisting the rifle onto my shoulder, I patted my belt. "Damn. If only I had brought an axe I could cut a couple of trees for a backdrop."

Following my tracks in reverse towards home, I needed to find trees with green boughs to create a shelter with. Coming into a vale of evergreen spruce as the sun was setting, I walked around the trees picking up branches and dragging them with me as I searched for a fallen tree or snag that would burn all night.

The cloudless sky, and a near full moon, made it easy to find fuel for a fire. "Lucky for me," I picked up a limb, tucking it under my arm, "I decided to run from my problems while the weather was good. An' let's hope it stays that way."

As the moon rose higher, the breeze picked up strength, moving shadows around and teasing my imagination. The moonlight, as it reflected off the snow, created an inverted image of daylight. It was as if the light came from the ground up. And the shadows, so black they seemed impenetrable. Yet, the icy cold world before me was beautiful.

Several wolves howled in the distance. Their mournful wail broke the tranquil silence, sending shivers down my spine. "Damn, that's not what I wanted to hear. I better grab more wood just in case they want to pay me a visit."

Gathering what I hoped to be enough firewood, I started a fire. Using the light from it, I constructed a domed shelter from evergreen branches to protect me from the wind. Satisfied that I would be safe, I snuggled down into a pile of boughs and smoked a cigarette while watching the snow melt in my cup.

The next morning rising up cold and stiff, I stirred the ashes with numb hands searching for embers to build another fire. Coercing a flame from the embers, I was able to warm my hands enough to undo my pants and relieve myself.

Standing just outside the shelter, watering down the snow, I noticed a set of new tracks. They weren't wolf or a fox. They were too big for a lynx. The center pad was the size of my palm. Tossing a bough from the shelter onto the fire, I followed the tracks. They made a loop, curving around to the backside of my windbreak. Whatever it was, scraped at the snow I had piled against the woven branch framework. Kneeling for a closer look at a paw print, I spread my fingers and could barely cover it. The image of an Amur tiger, like the one in the picture hanging in the old woman's house came to mind.

Fear gripped my gut. I've had to deal with anxiety from the unknown almost every day, but the thought of being eaten was something I couldn't handle. Throwing down the stick in my hand, I raced around the shelter to get the rifle. Shouldering my pack, I set off for the cabin leaving the fire to burn itself out.

No longer caring about breaking into a sweat and getting chilled, I huffed it out. And by late afternoon made it to the trail at the far end of our trapline. The anxiety of some tiger taking a bite out of me, dwindled as I traversed through the familiar area. Then seeing a half-eaten critter in one of the traps, my own stomach growled, 'feed me.'

Pawing through my pack while I kept walking. There was one small piece of dried fruit to be found. Shoving it in my mouth, along with a handful of snow, I picked up speed once more at the thought of a bowl of venison stew waiting for me in the cabin.

Smoke from the chimney drifted into view as I stepped onto the main trail beyond the outhouse. Exhausted, I sat down on a stump and lit a cigarette. "Well, I made it back one in piece. Hallelujah. At least in the spring, I'll know where the river is." Forcing myself to get up, I stumbled down the trail with thoughts of a hot meal in our little hovel in paradise. "Ah, yes, I must say I missed her cooking."

Kicking my snowshoes off to the side of the porch, I flung the door open and was greeted by Arek standing on the other side. "Where the hell have you been?"

Dismayed at his brash welcome, I clenched my teeth and brushed by him. Hanging the rifle on its pegs, I filled a mug with hot water. The warmth of the cup on my cold hands felt good. Taking a sip, I stared out the small window.

Arek rubbed his knuckles, watching me ignore him. He didn't wait long, "Well?"

Before I could answer, Katya screamed in the other room. Arek ran to her. I kicked the chair next to my bunk, spinning it around and dropped into it. "What's her fuckin' problem?"

His voice shaking, he hollered, "She's in labor."

"Shit," I tossed the cup on the table and jumped up reaching for the rifle. "I'll go get Babushka."

At the old woman's house, she kept dragging her feet at every turn. And out of frustration, I kept demanding, "Hurry up."

Her response was the same, every time. "It's her first. Don't worry, we have time."

After watching the old woman as she browsed through her collection of herbs, picking each one up, holding it to the light and inspecting it. Then laying it down, then picking up the previous one, a second or third time. I grabbed her arm, stopping her silly meandering through the pharmacy. "Look, it's not Katya I'm worried about. It's what Arek might do," I growled.

Laughing, she winked as she closed her bag. "Yes, sometimes the father needs more attention. Let's go."

CHAPTER NINE

Several weeks after the baby boy was born, Vasiy, accompanied the old woman and a few of the clan elders for a visit to our cabin. Taking the tea kettle out onto the porch to fill with fresh water from the barrel Arek had made, I was eager to have a conversation that didn't contain the word "baby" in it. I tried talking to any of them who'd listen as I came back in. But, the elders however, immediately jumped into their ancient ritual for newborns.

Starting at the door, they swept the floor with birch branches. The symbolism at first was hard to tell if they were covering their tracks or just sweeping the floor. Finished with the floor, they then broke the limbs and threw them one by one in the stove as they formed a circle around the child. When the circle was complete, they began stomping and chanting while moving around the child.

With everyone involved and no one to talk to, I leaned against the wall out of their way and lit a cigarette. Immediately, the oldest looking woman stomped her way over and snatched it out of my mouth. She sniffed the curling smoke. Frowing, she shook her head from side to side, then with a deft snap of her wrist, flicked the cigarette into the stove. Babushka smiled at me as the circle kept moving around the child. Rolling my eyes, I reached for another. Vasiy came over and put his hand on my lighter before I could strike it. "Don't. Tobacco smoke must not mingle with the sacred incense during this ritual."

I put the cigarette behind my ear. "What's the ritual suppose to do?"

Folding his arms, Katya's cousin leaned against the wall next to me. "It's suppose to protect the child from evil spirits."

"You believe that?"

"Naw." He coughed at the pungent odor from the burning herbs. "But, it's a tradition performed with the birth of every child."

"Good thing Stefon's not here." I swiped at a cloud of ritual smoke as it floated by my face. "He definitely would have lost it and tried putting a stop to any of it."

Eyes still locked on the ritual, Vasiy reached in his shirt pocket."Thanks for reminding me." He held out a folded piece of paper. "Stefon sent a note for you."

The kettle whistled as I took the note from his hand. Shoving it in my pocket I pushed away from the wall. "I'll make the tea, then go outside and have that smoke while I read it."

I held the first cup out to Vasiy. He shook his head, pointing to the elders. "Them first."

By now they were kneeling around the crib, so I placed the tray on the floor next to Babushka where she could see it and backed away. Pouring two more cups, I gave one to Vasiy before taking my coat from its hook and slipping out the door.

Outside on the steps, with my coat draped over my shoulders and the cup of tea between my feet, I lit my cigarette. Exhaling the smoke with a sigh, I stared at the folded paper in my hand while pondering, *Do I want to know? Or am I gunna be pissed cause he got himself arrested. No, think positive. He's found someone to cook for him and is having a great life with lots of sheep in his flock.*

I took another drag and gazed into the cloudless sky. "Thank you Herman for getting me on that train." Flicking the cigarette into the snow, I gave a deep sigh, "OK, now for Stefon's good news."

Unfolding the note, I picked up my hot tea and held it to my nose, letting the steam clear my head while reading it.

"My friend Kezel. I've prayed hard since becoming a priest to get a parish like this one. My prayers have been answered. In all my joy though, I miss having our philosophical discussions during the morning meal. The three of you should come join me. Arek, with his skills, would be able to get a job quickly in Lidoga, just a few kilometers away. I'm sure we could find something for you. There is a lot of work around here. Why, just this

morning, the Captain of a fishing trawler, home on leave, asked if I knew of a young man who didn't drink, could do what he's told, and could speak English. I told him about you. He is interested in meeting you. He said he doesn't care that you are a gypsy and have no experience at sea, as long as you can work. You will need to come here right away. He wants to meet...

Screaming, "Yes," I dropped the mug onto the steps and jumped up running into the house.

Vasiy smiled as he watched me come through the door waving the letter. Our guests stopped whispering amongst themselves and stared at me.

"You knew what it said?"

Vasiy nodded. "Stefon told me of the job offer when he handed it to me."

The grin on my face grew ear to ear. "You know what this means?" I asked the elder sitting on the floor closest to me. "A chance to work...a chance to go home." Patting him on the shoulder then shaking my fist. "Yes, I've been waiting for years to......wait a minute." My enthusiasm faded. Turning to Vasiy, I mumbled, "I don't have any papers."

His face grew troubled as he walked across the room mouthing the words, "What happened to them?"

"Remember?" Asking in a hushed tone as I glanced at the elders before turning my back to them. "We only had enough money for the other three. You said mine would cost more and take more time."

Vasiy closed his eyes. Pinching the bridge of his nose, he leaned closer, "I brought all four of them at the same time."

Clearing my throat through clenched teeth, we both turned simultaneously glaring at Arek. My Polish, 'friend', quickly diverted his eyes. Vasiy put his arm around my shoulder pulling me closer. "Your papers were in that box I handed you, the day Stefon left."

My face burned as I bit my lip glaring harder at Arek, then at Katya.

Babushka, getting off her knees, came over. Putting a finger to her lips, she whispered, "The baby's sleeping." Then wrapping her hands around my head, she pulled my head down next to her lips. "Remember. It is your family that protects you from yourself."

Straightening up and squinting at her, I snorted with contempt at her comment.

Quietly the elders began rising one by one to their feet, preparing to leave. Taking turns whispering in the sleeping child's ear, kissing Katya on both cheeks, and then patting Arek on the back before they stepped out onto the porch. Vasiy, the last one in line, looked at me as he helped the old woman on with her coat. "I'm heading towards Lidoga to pick up fuel in three days. Be at the drop off point if you decide to go."

Babushka patted my chest and gave me a grandmotherly smile. "Come see me before you go, Weasel."

"Yes ma'am. How else am I to learn what not to do?"

After the porch cleared and the door closed, I stood for a moment looking at the door. Taking a deep breath, I turned slowly and stared at my roommates. They avoided making eye contact with me as they straightened up the cabin. Struggling with my anger, I walked over to the stove and jerked its door open. Seizing the fire poker from under the firebox, acrid clouds of smoke wafted into the cabin each time I jabbed at the burning pile of wood. Taking a cigarette out of my pocket, I lit it with a glowing ember stuck to the tip of the iron tool. Dropping the poker onto the heart, I stared into the fire.

Arek, got up from the chair he was sitting in and went behind the curtain into their room. Angry at his leaving the room without speaking, I snatched a piece of wood off the stack and threw it into the firebox. It hit the backside and bounced halfway out. Losing control, I kicked the burning piece of wood into the stove and forced the door shut.

Arek stepped from behind the curtain and held out a folded identity card with several papers tucked inside. "Here, these are yours."

Stomping over and snatching them from of his hand, I studied each document carefully. Looking at the mix of handwritten and printed Cyrillic alphabet, I didn't fully understand what was written on the papers, and at the moment I don't care. I now have papers that give me an identity. The first step of getting the hell out of this country.

The stove started to rattle from the uncontrolled fire inside. Arek stepped past me and turned the air flow down. I glanced up from the papers. "When were you planning on giving me these?"

Gingerly, he flipped a small piece of bark on the floor with his toe. "I didn't find the papers until several weeks after we got the box. I...I wasn't sure when—"

"Sure of what?" I growled.

"Look, your friendship means a lot to me—"

"Oh really? By hiding my papers!" My voice rose several notches. "Is that what friends do in Poland?"

Katya stepped in between us. "It wasn't his idea, it was mine. I thought you would leave as soon as you got them."

"What the fuck!" I slapped the papers against my palm. "Who the hell are you, to tell me what I can or cannot do?"

"You don't know the mannerisms of the Russian people. And, well, I was afraid you'd get picked up. You mean a lot to me and Arek..." Katya looked down at the sleeping baby in her arms. "And we didn't want you to miss this."

"Humpft." I turned my back on her. Taking out a cigarette, I lit it. The baby coughed and started fussing. I crushed the unfinished cigarette on the stove and looked at the child. "You're right. Most likely I would have."

Arek put his arm around my shoulder. "We would like to name him after you. If that's OK?"

"I'm...I'm honored, but aren't you supposed to name him after someone in the family? Like Vasiy. Or even a fellow countryman like Stefon?"

Katya threw an arm around me and the two gave me a hug. "You are family," she said. "Stefon will get the next one."

CHAPTER TEN

The morning of me leaving for Stefon's, I sat on the porch in the early morning darkness with a cup of tea and a cigarette, thinking of Tomas and his excuses of why he didn't want to escape with me to America. His logic of those around him had become his family, suddenly made sense.

After the sun rose, I double checked to make sure I had Tomas's wallet, his letter to his mother, and his watch. Stepping back inside the cabin and setting my cup on the table, I announced, "OK, I think I'm ready."

Katya gave me a hug then disappeared into her room.

Arek lifted the rifle from its hooks. "Just in case."

I waved my hand toward the door. "And, just in case... after you."

"You still don't trust me, do you?"

"It's more... I like hearing what's going on around me."

Chuckling, he threw his arm around my shoulder pulling me out the door. "Let's go, before you change your mind."

As promised, we stopped by Babushka's house, knowing I had to be careful if she started one of her stories. Still, I felt obligated to stay long enough to have at least one cup of tea.

Babushka, pouring her thick sweet tea into the cups set before us, began to speak of when her son had left to seek work in another part of the country.

Wrapping my hands around the steaming cup, I sat up straight. *Be careful...This is beginning to sound familiar.*

By the time I finished with my tea, her son had still not left the village. Divided between hearing the end of her story, or being rude and rushing out the door,I looked at my watch. Arek, noticing my restlessness, leaned over, "Don't worry, he'll wait. Besides, you don't know if the time on that thing is right."

Babushka paused her story long enough to refill our cups. Sitting down, she began her slow, meticulous dialog once more. Leaning over, I grabbed a handful of snow from the bucket sitting next to the stove and dropped it in my tea. She stopped talking and watched me down the drink in one swallow. Nodding, the old woman put her cup down and reached for a small leather pouch lying on the table in front of her. Taking out a necklace, she held it up. "I want you to have this." Her eyes moistened. "It will protect you, and give you strength over your enemies."

A tiger's-eye stone hung in the center, with two large fangs suspended on each side of the center stone. My jaw dropped at seeing the size of those teeth. "I can't take what belongs to your son, it—"

"Hush, child." She rose to her feet. "My son visited you that night above the river. He said you will need this where you are going."

Confused, I was speechless. I didn't tell anyone of what happened that night. How could she have known?

"Since the beginning of my people, this has been known as the...Eye of the Tiger. It is said... *'No man who looks into the eyes of a tiger, shall live to tell the story'*. Wear it, my child, and you will share their powers... the stealth and cunning of a tiger. No one will be able to stand against you."

"But, shouldn't—"

"Hush, it is you who is to wear it." Babushka placed the amulet around my neck while whispering in her native tongue. Kissing me on the cheek, she left the room before I could protest any further.

I caressed the amulet. My insides churned at the new responsibilities of caring for a piece of Evenki culture.

Arek stood up. "It's time to leave."

Stepping onto the path at the bottom of her porch stairs, I picked up a stone and threw it at a tree. "You motherfucker, Tomas." I snatched up a second and threw it at a different tree. "Damn it to hell. It's not me who should be wearing this."

Arek stepped beside me placing his hand on my back. "Let's go before Vasiy gets tired of waiting."

"Yeah." I took a step and slipped on a piece of ice. Sprawled out on my back in the snow, I looked up at Arek. "Some talisman. Didn't even protect me on my first step."

At the meeting point, Vasiy pulled a box of supplies from his truck while I gave my comrade and brother, one final hug goodbye. "Take care of your family."

He nodded in silence.

I walked around and climbed in the passenger side of the truck.

As Vasiy opened his door to get in, I yelled across the cab over the noise of the diesel engine, "I won't forget you guys! I'll be back!"

* * *

The village that Stefan's church was nestled in had no official name. It was more of a conglomeration of dwellings in a broad meadow behind a gas station roadhouse. Not more than a thirty minute drive from the city of Lidoga.

Vasiy pulled into the traveler's stop and pointed at the wooden structures behind it. "That's his parish. You'll find him at the church in the middle of those houses."

"Where?" I stared out the window. "I don't see a dome or spire."

"You won't," he said as he pushed open his door and slid out. "It wasn't built to be a church. But, it is the tallest structure in the middle of the village."

Reaching behind his seat, he pulled a small box from its hiding spot and and closed his door leaving me alone. As I watched Vasiy disappear from sight, Katya's comments about my ability to blend in as a native Russian suddenly unnerved me and I just sat there looking around. *This sure seems like an odd place to meet a fishing captain. There's no ocean, no river.*

A herd of cows mooing in the meadow across the road jarred the memory of crossing the meadows during our escape from the gulag. Smiling, I mimicked a Drill Sargent I had in Basic Training, "Yo' momma ain't here to do it fo' ya, so, get yo' ass moving, maggot." I pushed open the door and jumped out. Taking my bag and slamming the truck door shut, I looked at the yellow gravel pathway towards town. *OK, just follow the yellow brick road...oh my.*

Taking a step, I started to whisper, "Follow the yellow brick road...oh my!" over, and over, as I walked across the graveled parking lot. At the grassy edge, and shifting gears, I tossed my bag over my shoulder, clenched an unlit cigarette between my teeth to keep from smiling, and hurried along the walkway.

Standing at the foot of its front steps, I glanced up and down the street. *Vasiy was right. The building is, in the center of the village, and, it is the tallest. But, man, I've never seen such a plain church.*

"Well..." I muttered, spitting the cigarette out of my mouth. "Let's get it over with."

Cautiously climbing the three steps to the front door, I reached for the door knocker. As my fingers touched the iron ring, the unlatched door swung inward. Still not confident I was in the right spot, I pushed the door open further for a better view inside. It didn't look like a church entrance, but then, it didn't exactly look like a hotel either.

Stepping into the foyer, to the right, there were stairs going up to a second floor. Straight ahead, a double-door opened into what looked like a gymnasium. Walking into the gym and looking along the walls, they were covered with a simple map of the USSR, crude children's drawings of fish, pictures of people working nets in a river, and a portrait of Prime Minister Brezhnev. A smell of fish came from two wet spots under the children's drawings. Past the Prime Minister, was pictures of Chinese Emperors, dragons, pandas and calligraphy. The pungent aroma of sandalwood incense hung around a table placed under the pandas.

The third wall, had a lone icon of the Virgin Mary, along with a small table with a single candle under her picture. The wall with the entrance door, had photographs of ordinary citizens working. Some standing next to trucks, some in uniforms, and others were just portraits. Two small tables under those photos held a dozen or so burning candles. "This can't be the church," I whispered turning around looking from wall to wall again. "What the heck is this place?"

Stefon stepped in behind me. "But it is, my friend."

Greeting him with a hug, I smirked, "It doesn't look like one to me."

"Actually, it's our community center," he said pointing toward Brezhnev's picture. "It's also school for seven young children." He put his arm around my shoulder, squeezing me. "And yes...I am one of the teachers."

With his arm still around my shoulder, he guided me towards one of the tables with burning candles. "The other teacher is a very fine young woman. After my own heart, I would say."

"Wait a minute, priests can't...you know."

Stefon patted my shoulder before he leaned over the burning candles. "I'm not a priest." Plucking several candle remnants from their glass holders, he grinned, "At least not officially."

Taking a new candle from a box under the table, he placed it below the picture of Vasiy. "And this...this is our memorial to those who were, and to those who—"

The sound of the outer door shutting, reverberated in the gym.

A burly, dark-haired man stepped in through the inner door and made silent eye contact with Stefon then walked over to the map. Stefon watched the stranger for a second, then motioning me towards the foyer, he whispered, "Upstairs is our flat, where you'll be staying. Make us a cup of tea, will you please?"

Walking upstairs and following the short hallway, I walked past the open bathroom door. *All right, inside plumb—*

Backing up and taking a second look at something unusual that caught my eye. There were nylons, panties, and bras hanging on a drying rack in the bath tub. Shaking my head and wrinkling my nose, I whispered, "Here we go again."

In the kitchen, shedding my coat, I threw it at the radiator next to the wall. Free of the extra weight and rubbing my hands together with anticipation of an easier life style, I scanned the counters for the teapot. Instead of a teapot, the under-counter refrigerator jumped out at me. "Yes." My fingers slipped around its handle. The small door swung open, exposing nearly empty shelves. "Damn, no O J or pie." Giving a disappointed sigh, I closed the fridge.

There it was, sitting on a back burner, empty. The black kettle blended in with the gas cooktop. "This is going to be such a gravy train. Take it to the sink...fill it from a faucet. Ohh baby, no...more...buckets."

With the kettle filled and on the stove, a new challenge suddenly presented itself. How to turn the gas on. I bent over examining the faint markings behind the valves I assumed were the control knobs. Engrossed in my confused effort to decipher the rubbed out lettering, I didn't hear the footsteps coming up behind me. "You must be the friend Stefon was expecting?"

Her soft voice startled me. I straightened up and tried twisting one of the lever-type knobs. "How do you turn this on?"

"Push in and turn."

The burner didn't light. "Do you know if the pilot light is lit on this thing?"

"You have to hold a match to the burner."

"Oh." I struck my lighter and held it close. The flame jumped. "Should have known it would be something that simple."

Sliding the kettle onto the burner, I turned facing the voice. Her smile accented her slender features and long beet-red hair. She definitely was not what I expected as Stefon's type. Feeling my face getting warmer the longer I looked at her, I finally shook my head and answered, "Uhm...yes, I am."

She stepped next to the stove and reached up on a shelf taking down a tin of biscuits. Placing them on the table she went to another cupboard and took out three cups. "Did you bring your wife?"

Captivated with her gracefulness, I mumbled, "Uhmm, that's our other friend, Arek."

"Oh." Putting the fourth cup in her hand back onto the shelf, she turned towards the table.

I held out my hand. "I'm Kezel."

She glanced at my hand and smiled as she walked by. " Mine's Sasha." Sitting down, Sasha shuffled the cups around. "So you're the, gypsy, Stefon holds in such high esteem."

Her emphasis on the word, gypsy, pricked me. Opening my mouth to give her a snarky response, the kettle whistled distracting me. I turned and grabbed it, answering, "Yes, I am."

Placing the teapot on the hot pad in front of her, I whirled my hand in the air emphasizing my question. "And you be what?"

Her tone chilled even more. "Moldavian."

"Don't worry, sister," I laughed as I leaned over the table to grab a cookie, "I won't steal your children. Or belongings."

Her face went pale and she covered her eyes. "Put it away. Please!"

I looked down at my zipper, then at her. "What are you talking about?"

"Put it away!"

"Put what away?"

She patted her chest. "The talisman."

Without knowing it, the necklace had slipped outside of my shirt. Feeling the tiger's teeth dangling, I slipped them back inside. "Superstitious, eh?"

She peeked between her fingers. "It's not superstition!"

"Uh huh, right."

"That's what I thought too, when I came here. Then I did some research, just to prove my point to the children." Picking up her spoon, she stirred a cube of sugar into her tea. "When the Chinese controlled the Amur Valley many generations ago. There was a shaman of the Evenki people who claimed he could talk to the tigers. He said the tigers gave him that amulet as a sign of their brotherhood. For reasons unknown, anyone who opposed the shaman was killed by a tiger." The look on her face was one of dead seriousness.

"They're children's stories." Picking up my cup, I grinned. "Besides, what makes you think this the same one?"

"I know it is." She took a biscuit from the plate and held it up. "There are drawings of it around the shaman's neck." Waving the biscuit at me, her eyes narrowed. "And that looks exactly like it."

Taking a cigarette out and tapping it on the table, I looked her in the eye. "Legends are known to provide answers when there aren't any to be found." I stopped tapping and glanced around for an ashtray. "Besides, that happened hundreds of years ago."

"When the Czar conquered the valley, the killings kept happening." Her voice became more intense. "When the Bolsheviks took control, it became their turn. When the Japanese invaded during the war, tigers killed many of them, too."

"What do you expect?" I laid the cigarette on the table and leaned back in my chair. "Tigers live here."

"Yes, they do, but each one of those who died, had an argument with a shaman wearing that talisman. But with the Japanese...they were trying to drive the Evenki out of the valley."

Hearing footsteps on the stairs as I was about to chide her logic, I bit my tongue and sat upright. Suddenly two hands began rubbing the back of my shoulders. "I see you've met Sasha." Stefon stepped around me and greeted her with a kiss on the cheek.

"Yes," I smiled as he slipped into the chair between us. "She's been giving me quite a history lesson."

He reached over, placing his hands on hers. "Isn't she a fabulous teacher?"

"I'm happy for you." Rising from my chair, I walked over to my bag and pulled out a book-size package. I set it on the table before him. "Babushka wanted me to give you this."

He drew back like I had placed a snake in front of him. "No! It couldn't be." That was followed by a smile exploding across his face. "She often talked about them, but I never actually saw any of them." Delicately he removed the cloth wrappings of his gift, revealing two icons of the Madonna. "Her father saved these from the purge during the revolution."

"Well, preacher man," dropping into my chair, I leaned back. "You'll just have to say a prayer for grandma as a thank you."

Glancing over at Sasha, the numb look on her face puzzled me. It wasn't until Stefon placed the pictures side by side, that she reached over and touched one of the wooden panels, softly sliding her fingers along its edge.

Not understanding his reverence for the artwork, I poured myself another cup of tea and picked up my cigarette from the table. Stefon stretched behind Sasha, grabbed an ashtray from the counter, placing it on the table in front of me. "Thank you, my friend, for bringing us these precious gifts."

As the smoke from my cigarette drifted over the table, he draped the cloth wrapping over the pictures. Picking up his cup, he leaned on his elbows. "How's Arek and his family?"

Sasha stifled a cough before rising to her feet.

I watched her go over to the sink and fidget with a couple of dirty dishes. "I don't know how he gets along with that woman," I answered in a snarky tone as I snubbed out the cigarette.

"What about the child?" Stefon tapped his fingers on the table in an effort to get my attention. "Was it a boy or girl?"

Sitting with my eyes focused on the ashtray, I nodded. "It was a boy." Then grinning and wiping at a few ashes from the table, I looked him in the eye. "It definitely has changed him though."

"Oh praise God." Stefon clapped his hands. "I'm hoping they'll move here. There's plenty of work if he wants it."

"If you remember? That's why I came here."

Stefon put his finger to his lips and nodded toward Sasha. "We'll talk about it later."

Prison had taught me well that open conversations within earshot of other individuals, often had consequences. Glancing at Sasha, I crossed my arms and leaned further back in my chair. "I think if you told Arek there was electricity and steam heat, he'd pack up his family and be on your doorstep tomorrow."

Stefon chuckled as he picked up my lighter studying the etchings on it. "I almost kissed the radiator when I arrived. I praise God every day for the wonders of modern life."

"I—" My tilted chair slipped on the linoleum, dropping me hard on my back.

Laughing so hard tears ran down his cheeks, Stefon struggled with his words, "You...should...have...seen...your face."

Catching my breath I began howling with laughter, too.

Sasha, looked over at us, then went back to peeling vegetables without so much as a smile.

"Damn." I wiped my eyes with my sleeve then slowly rolled onto my side. "And to think, I haven't had anything to drink." Snapping my fingers, I crawled over to my bag. "I brought another gift. This one from Katya." Pulling a bottle of vodka from the rucksack, I placed it on the table. With a quick hook of my foot, I hoisted my chair up and grabbed its back, setting it by the table. "Katya wanted me to take both bottles. But I reminded her, a house without vodka is not a house, but a hovel."

Cracking open the bottle, I poured a swallow into Stefon's cup, then mine. Gazing at my Polish friend, I sucked in a deep breath and raised my cup. "To Zarkhov! Had it not been for the asshole, we may never have made it as far as we did."

Stefon raised his drink and snarled, "May the bastard rot in hell."

"Whoa!" Surprised by his vindictive attitude, I held my drink still. "Where did that come from?"

With his cup at his lips, he glanced at me. Nodding, he lowered it, "You're right." Suddenly raising it above his head, he bellowed, "Praise God for all we have." Then downed the drink and slammed his cup on the table.

I followed suit.

Sasha walked over and half-ass flung a bowl of salad greens on the table. "I hope you don't plan on keeping this up all night." Spinning on her heels, she walked back to the stove.

I sneered at her backside and smacked the table with my palm. "I don't care for your insinuation. For one thing, I'm not a damn Russian—."

"Kezel, that's enough." Stefon shoved his cup further across the table. "We need to be compassionate towards other people's feelings."

Sasha diverted her eyes away from us when she returned with a platter of fish. Silently preparing herself a plate, she took it over by the television on the other side of the room. Turning on the black and white television set, she flopped on the couch with the sound up loud enough to drown out anything said at the table.

Stefon leaned forward. "I'll send word to the captain tomorrow. He seemed extremely eager to meet you when I mentioned you were a gypsy from Germany and could speak English. Not in a bad way, but more in a positive thought."

I nodded at his comment. Not that I really heard what he said, but because my attention was glued to the TV. It had been years since I'd seen a television, along with never seeing a Russian broadcast before.

Stefon stood up and grabbed the vodka, pouring each of us another shot, he twisted the cap back on.

I looked up at him. Then over at her, and then at the vodka in my cup.

"Don't worry, I'll take care of her." He raised his drink, "May God bless you my friend."

I tapped his cup, "Here, here." Downing the swallow of clear liquid then pouring myself another, I raised my cup and nodded toward Sasha. "To your happiness."

CHAPTER ELEVEN

The captain seemed pleasant and unassuming while sitting at our kitchen table conducting his interview. He told Stefon he wanted it to be very informal, as it was his custom of doing things. I was still taken aback at his insistence I make us a snack and a pot of tea while asking me questions.

Most of his questions were generic in fashion, inquiring about my knowledge of ships, my labor skills. Did I speak English? Had I been around Americans while living in Germany? Had I been sent to prison in Siberia? Which one, and why? The longer the interview went on, the more it appeared he was probing to see if I would jump ship in a foreign port?

Done with his questioning, he closed his book and asked that I stand in front of him with my feet spread apart, and hold out my right hand. Taking hold of my hand, he pushed it away, then pulled it inward. "That one seems strong enough. Now hold out your left."

Holding out my left hand, my sleeve slid up exposing the tattoo on my forearm. He paused, then pressed his finger on it, studying the artwork. With a strange smile, he let go of my hand and turned around to the table. Flipping open his notebook, he took a folded form from its inner pocket, studied it for a moment, then held it out to me. Cautiously, I reached for the papers.

He rubbed his mustache with his finger as he spoke. "Seven days from now, we leave from the third pier in Vanino. Be there in five."

I gawked at the paper, excited at the opportunity for a ride...right up to America's doorstep. In the meantime, without waiting for so much as a thank you, he picked up his book and walked down the stairs. Hearing the door open brought me out of my daze. I ran to the top of the stairs in time to see his arm close the outside door, I whispered in English, "Thank you."

Sasha stepped into the foyer from the great room. She looked up at me. "Who was that?"

"Oh, no one." I folded the paper in my hands and shoved it under my shirt. "He came up to let us know we were out of candles at the alter."

She came up the stairs, glancing out the window at his vehicle pulling away. I emptied the ashtray into a rubbish bin, then set it in the sink. Seeing the two cups and dirty plate on the table, she gave me a quizzical look. I grabbed what was left of the biscuits on the plate and brushed past her, disappearing into my room.

Music blasting from a phonograph along with the stomping of little feet on the wooden floor below, woke from my nap. Pulling on a shirt, I went into the kitchen, turned on the stove and made some tea.

Sauntering down the stairs with a cup of tea in hand, I stood in the foyer watching the commotion. Sasha had the children in a circle doing some kind of exercise, while Stefon struggled to set up a blackboard on a tripod behind them. The children's stomping didn't help much. The chalk in its tray, kept bouncing onto the floor breaking into smaller and smaller pieces. Snickering at the sight of Stefon trying to keep the chalk in the tray, I nearly missed the sound of a truck stopping in front the building.

Turning and peeking out the window, I could see a delivery van had pulled up. Nothing unusual, people always stopped during their work to say a prayer and light candles. Only, something didn't look right this time. The driver wore a familiar, knee-length black leather coat. I stepped closer to the window to get a better view. Several more men emerge from the back of the van, all wearing the same black coat. "Their coats look an awful lot like Zark—"

Spinning around and yelling, "Chekas!" to Stefon thru the inner door, I grabbed my boots from their place in the foyer and ran up the stairs with the intention of hightailing it out the back door. In the middle of the kitchen, I looked at the windows remembering there wasn't a door and the windows were too small to climb out. I was trapped.

Tossing the boots over by the couch, I ran into the bathroom, wrapped a towel around my neck, then smeared shaving soap on my face. Covered with foam, I started searching for a razor. The sound of hard-heeled boots as they climbed the wooden stairs echoed up the stairwell. My heart pounded with each step of the Cheka's slow cadence,...thud...thud...thud....

I wanted to scream, *Where the fuck is that razor,* as I searched the shelf above the sink. The footsteps, reaching the top of the stairs, began a slow walk down the hallway. Much like a hunter, stalking his prey, waiting for it to flush.

Knocking a bottle of pills into the sink, I snatched the bottle from the dry basin, *Oh shit, fill the damn thing, you dipshit.*

I jammed the drain plug in place and before I could turn the water on, the footsteps stopped. Gripping the free-standing sink with both hands, the hair on the back of my neck tingled, causing me to shudder. Slowly I raised my eyes, looking in the mirror towards the door. A black coated figure stared back at me.

I leaned towards the mirror pretending he was just an ordinary Joe. "This area is a private residence. Do you mind?"

The man's face was cold and empty of emotion as he asked, "Is anyone else up here?"

"Like I said, the community center is downstairs." I resumed searching for a razor.

Folding his arms across his chest in a menacing fashion, he repeated, "Is anyone else up here?"

I glared at him in the mirror. "No."

"What are you doing?" His body language suggested he wouldn't take anything less than a submissive answer. Pushing aside the curtain that hung from the front of a cabinet next to the sink, I pawed among the items on its shelf. "Shaving...that is if I can find the razor."

Glancing at him in the mirror, nothing but his eyes moved as he watched me search. Picking up the soap cup, I pulled the brush out and stirred the foam with my fingers.

"It's on the floor," he snapped.

I looked down at my feet. "Oh."

"Your papers!"

Motioning with my soapy hand towards the hall, I sputtered, "In my coat."

He stepped back away from the door and waited.

The soap, now running down my neck, I let it go and wiped my hands. Retrieving the papers out of my jacket hanging on the coat rack at the top of the stairs, I held them out. The agent snatched them from my hand. Opening my identity booklet, he held it up to my face. His eyes glared at the photo, then at me.

My fears began to give way to annoyance as the shaving soap trickled past the towel and down my chest. Closing the identity card, he unfolded my travel permit. After reading it he glared at me. "How come it's not stamped?"

"I arrived...phfft," I daubed at the foam running across my lips, "yesterday after the office was closed. I was preparing to report as soon as I finished cleaning up." Brushing at the foam under my shirt with the towel, I gave him a toothy grin, "That was until you gentlemen interrupted me from doing my responsibility. I hope you won't take much longer, I would—"

His steely eyes stopped my babbling.

Glancing over my shoulder down the stairs, I whispered, "Who you looking for? Maybe I can help."

"Escaped prisoners," he sneered, slapping my papers against my chest so hard his knuckles left marks.

Point taken, I took the papers, shoving them into my back pocket.

He went into the open living room-kitchen area and began scanning the room like he had x-ray vision. Apparently satisfied that what he wanted wasn't there, he returned to the hall and walked past me into Sasha's bedroom.

I stood in the doorway watching as he pocketed Sasha's perfume. I gritted my teeth and twisted the towel around my neck as he opened her dresser drawers, going through her clothes. Finding nothing else to steal, he walked into the hall and over to my door. "What's in this room?"

"It's my room." I twisted the knob and pushed the door open.

Sticking his head in, he nodded. Spinning on his heels, he pushed past me and went down the stairs. Standing next to the hand railing, I tried listening to the Cheka's muted conversation in the foyer.

One, by one, they walked out the front door. When the last one left, Stefon went to the door and closed it. He stood there, staring at their van through the lace curtains covering the window. Watching the van from the window at the top of the stairs, I glanced down at Stefon, "What do you think?"

"I'm not sure."

When the van finally started and left, I went down the stairs and stood next to Stefon as he continued staring out at the empty street. Hearing a child sniffle, I looked over at Sasha. She was sitting on the floor in the middle of the great room, rocking several of the children. I whispered, "I don't—"

Stefon tapped the glass in the window, "They are like wolves that have smelled blood. They'll be back."

"I need to leave then," I wiped the soap off my face with the towel. "But I don't have money for a ticket."

Stefon looked at me. "What?"

I shrugged. "Hey, I wasn't expecting to leave so fast. I left all the cash with Arek and only brought the jewelry and a few furs, figuring I'd have time to sell 'em here."

"I'll see what I can do." He opened the door and walked out.

Closing the door, I ran upstairs into the kitchen. Grabbing the bottle of vodka from the shelf, I chugged a stiff drink. My throat burning, I cursed about it under my breath and shoved the bottle back onto the shelf. Leaning against the table lighting a cigarette, I tried to gather my thoughts.

"What are you going to do?"

Bristling at the sound of her voice, I glared at her.

Sasha stepped back. "It wasn't me."

I ground out my cigarette in the ashtray and brushed past her. Following me into my room, she watched as I knelt and pulled my bag from under the bed. Opening the bag I pulled two wolf pelts from it. As I unrolled them she gasped, "They're beautiful."

"Tell me," I snarled. "I need to sell them so I can get outta here."

Gently stroking their fur, she whispered, "I'll buy them."

"You don't have shit, woman." I rolled one up, tucking it back in the bag. "You couldn't afford one, let alone both of them."

"I can too! I'll give you three hundred for both," she insisted.

"You have kids downstairs. Go."

"No, really. I have the money."

"Go away!" I demanded as I left going to the living room to find a newspaper.

Stefon came in the front door and bounded up the stairs. Sasha stood at the top looking at him through moist eyes. Taking hold of her hands and kissing them, he nodded towards the downstairs. Following me back into my room, Stefon closed the door. "There's a place in Lidoga that buys furs." He held out a piece of paper. "Here's the address."

Catching a glimpse of the writing as I took it from his hand, "I can't read this, it's in Polish."

Taking a deep breath, he snatched it away from me and went to the kitchen table.

I grabbed the bag of jewelry I had hid under some cloths on the floor and followed. Tossing it on the table next to him as he re-wrote the address, I asked, "What do you think I can get for these?"

Dumping out the bag on the table, he picked up a woman's plain gold band, "I'll give you ten for this one."

"Take it." I slipped the address in my pocket. "All I need is enough for a ticket to the coast."

He scooped up the rest of the jewelry, putting it in his pocket. "I think I know someone who can help."

Surprised at Stefon's willingness to fence stolen goods, I watched him disappear out the door. Looking over at the clock on the wall and seeing it was mid-afternoon, I sat down at the table listening to the sound of the children's parents picking them up.

When the last one finally left, I jumped out of my chair. "Perfect. They're gone."

Standing in front of the large map, I stared at a useless black and white picture of the USSR. Essentially, it reminded me of a large piece of butcher paper with an outline of the country. A few cities were named, the largest rivers were indicated, and a number of the motorways were drawn in straight-line fashion, along with the lone Trans-Siberian Railroad. "Damn paranoid commies," I bitched in English while walking over to the bus and train schedules posted in the foyer.

Sasha came into the foyer, standing behind me as I scanned the schedules. "I have the money to buy those furs."

"No." I continued sliding my finger down the list of cities. "I'm not selling them to you."

"Why?"

"No. How do I know you're not conning me on the price?"

"But, Ke—"

"No."

Grabbing my arm, she whined, "What will it take to convince you?"

Agitated, I turned, glaring into her eyes. "Sex!"

Her eyes fluttered and her face blushed as she stammered, "Ah...ah—"

I cut her off. "My way, all night. Plus the three hundred."

Tears flowing down her cheeks, she ran to her desk in the corner of the great room and buried her head in her arms. Satisfied I had won the argument and that she wouldn't bother me again, I went upstairs.

Throwing my notes on the table, I went to the kitchen sink and prepared a fresh pot of water for tea. Lighting the burner and a cigarette with the same match, I leaned against the sink thinking of Masha, wondering what my life would have been like had she lived. She knew who I was, better than I did myself.

Miserable with emotions of losing her, I took Tomas's watch out of my pocket and began winding it. Instead of easing the pain, it brought Tomas's wretched death in my arms replaying before my eyes. Shuddering, I raised my face to the ceiling and screamed, "The two people I cared for the most...on the same fucking day. Why didn't I? WHY?" Closing my eyes, it was all I could do to take a breath.

The whistling kettle cut through the fog and brought me back to the kitchen. Bitterness and contempt revived my desire to get out of Russia before another friend died. In my anger fueled carelessness, I snatched the kettle off the burner sloshing hot water down my pant leg. "Mother fuck, you asshole." Tossing the kettle into the sink, I hobbled over to the table and brushed at my pant leg. *That's all you need to do, is burn yourself so you can't get the ship on time.*

Dropping into a chair, I wiped my nose on my sleeve and closed my eyes.

"Kezel." Stefon touched my shoulder. "Kezel, wake up."

Raising my head, it felt worse than any hangover I'd ever had. I mumbled, "How'd you do?"

He sat down. "God is looking out for you." Placing a pile of bank notes on the table next to my hand, he patted them as he announced, "One hundred rubles."

I knew the jewelry had to be worth at least three times that much, but, he was my friend. I took half the stack. "A bus ticket to Lidoga is only five rubles, you keep the other half."

"No, no. That is your half. My half is here." He patted his shirt pocket.

Gathering the stack of bills from the table, I glanced over in the kitchen and saw Sasha cutting vegetables. Weighing the stack in my hand, I reached over and patted his shirt pocket. "Now I'm positive that it is I, who's converted you."

"How do mean?"

"Maybe we should buy you a tambourine and a head scarf." I folded the bills and tapped them on the table. "Possibly a gold earring, too."

Stefon laughed at my poor joke.

"God is very generous in answering prayers," Sasha quipped.

Ignoring her, I shoved the money in my hip pocket, "Thank you, Stefon." Settling back in my chair, I caught a glimpse of my boots that I had tossed earlier. "I could use some new boots. Maybe rain gear, too."

Sasha brought the plates and silverware over to the table and set them before me, then went back to the meal she was cooking. Taking a deep breath after looking at the clock on the wall, I exhaled and picked up the plates placing them around the table. "Too late to go now, the last bus just left. I'll have to go in the morning."

Stefon fetched three glasses from the cupboard and followed behind Sasha as she carried supper to the table. Sitting, they bowed their heads in unison. After saying grace, Stefon poured what was left of the vodka into the three glasses. He took the middle one and held it aloft. "May you get home safely." I reached over taking the closest one and raised it, "May friends not be forgotten." I watched Sasha for her reactions. She slowly reached over and took the last one, "May we always be friends." Tapping the cups together, we drank their contents then proceeded to eat the meal in silence.

After supper, Stefon and I went downstairs to clean the great room. Grabbing several of the chairs he started to stack them, then paused, "Kezel...in all of my life, I have never been on a boat out of sight of land. I'm not sure I could do it."

I took an eraser and tried wiping the chalk board. "Neither have I, but at least I won't have to worry about the Cheksky,"

"They are everywhere, my friend. Don't fool yourself." Sliding the stack of chairs next to a closet and then reaching in and pulling out a push-broom, he began to sweep the floor. "And should the ship go to a foreign port, they'll rattle that chain around your neck."

"I'm hoping we make a foreign port. Especially an American one."

He stopped pushing his broom. "You know...that in your country, you are a 'persona non grata', yes? So how would you get the necessary papers to move about?"

"Not a problem, we don't need papers." Picking up a trash can, I emptied it into another. "Oh yeah...I will need a driver's license."

"And how will you do that, my friend? You are dead in the eyes of your government. And they have most likely convinced everyone of that, too." Stopping in the middle of the floor, he leaned on the broom, "With all that in mind, why leave? You're family here."

"Haw! That's what Tomas said to me. And look at what happened to him." Dropping the trashcan in my hands next to a table with burning candles, I chided him, "Besides, I thought you were going to free Poland."

"That's going to change." He gathered the dirt he had swept up into a dust pan and began walking towards me. "How soon, I can not say, but it's going to happen soon."

Picking a match-like stick from its cup, I held it over the flame of a candle. "There is no way you are going to convince me that that's going to happen." Using the match to light another candle, I placed it under Vasiy's picture.

"What makes you think that it won't?"

"Remember what you did in Prague?" Picking up another candle, I lit it. "Moscow will do the same in Warsaw."

Tossing the sweepings into the trashcan, he offered, "May I light a candle and pray that you have a safe journey?"

"Sure." I pulled out a cigarette and pointed it at him. "Between your prayers and Babushka's talisman, it should be a walk in the park to get home."

He shoved the trashcan under the table and sighed, "Aaaah, I miss her cooking."

Nodding in agreement, I quietly followed him up the stairs. At the top, he went to the kitchen, and I to my room.

* * *

Waking from the movement of the mattress, I laid still as someone slid under the covers next to me. In the dark of the night I could tell who it was by their scent. Pressing gently up against my back, she began to kiss my neck.

"No. You have to leave," I whispered.

Pulling herself closer and pressing her breasts firmly against my bare back, I turned over to face her. "No. I won't," I whispered placing my hand on her ribs and pushing her away.

The softness of her flesh enticed my carnal desires. The more I touched her, the weaker my will to resist became. In a lame effort, I tried sliding away. A step ahead of me, she pushed me onto my back and quickly climbed on top. Pressing her lips to mine, she slipped her hand under my shorts. At that point I caved.

* * *

Awaking later than anticipated the next morning, I got dressed in a hurry. Reaching under the bed for my bag with the wolf pelts. I found the bag empty, with a pile of money on top. Dumping it on the bed, I counted the cash. "What do you know, she did have it."

I stuffed most of the paper bills in the bottom of my boots and tossed the handful of coins on the bed, leaving her a tip. Stepping into the hallway, I caught her lingering scent. My stomach tightened as I walked towards the kitchen, *Damn her, that was not supposed to happen.*

Stefon, sitting at the table, had a stack of papers in front of him. Pouring myself a cup of tea, I pulled up a chair. He mumbled a good morning as he focused on sorting the stack into two piles. Struggling with the guilt of betraying my friend, I silently leaned back in my chair smoking a cigarette while watching him.

Unable to stand his silence any longer, I asked, "What are you doing?"

"These are the children's papers." He said as he continued sorting them. "I'm getting them ready."

Nodding, I waited for him to say something about Sasha. Instead, he stayed centered on his sorting. Slowly, I sipped my tea and wound Tomas' watch.

Stefon finally held up the last one, studied it, then placed it on a stack. Looking over at me, he sighed, "That's done."

"OK, what's goin' on?"

He slid back in his chair with a somber look on his face. "Remember when we first met on that train? How I said I wanted to go back home and help break the shackles of communism?"

I lit my third cigarette since sitting at the table. "Yeah. How can I forget?"

"Well. Sasha showed me that was the wrong way to go about it. It's extremely hard to change an adult's mind. So..." he held up the stacks, "if we teach the children to spurn the shackle...that will bring change to the system."

"That's great," I smiled. "So, where does the church fit in?"

Not being his usual jovial self, he sat there staring at me. Getting the impression that he knew about last night and was now going to lay into me, I gripped the edge of the table preparing for whatever he dished out.

Instead, he picked up the salt shaker and poured some into his hand. "The Soviets are atheists. They are like salt that has lost its flavor." He shook the granules from his palm. Then pouring more onto his hand, he continued, "Replace them with a new generation that despises communism and the church will grow."

Relieved, and thankful I still had all my teeth, I looked over at the clock. "I think your on the right track. That's better than protesting and going to prison. In fact..." rising to my feet and grabbing my bag, I looked at him, "would you mind walking me to the bus stop?"

CHAPTER TWELVE

An early spring rise in temperatures over the three days I had been at Stefon's, had caused severe flooding along the bus' route. There was so much water, it was flowing over the surface of the bridges. Where sections of the roadway had washed away, the bus, edging over in order to avoid a possible head-on collision, kept sliding into the ditch. Each time it did, the driver informed us it was our duty to get off and push it back onto the roadway.

Everyone seemed to take it in stride, and the fact that a thirty minute ride was now taking over an hour and a half left no one grumbling. Everything changed once the bus pulled into the station at Lidoga, then the other passengers fought like cats and dogs to get off.

Entering the bus station packed with jostling military troops in grey uniforms, green uniforms of the State Security (a branch of the KGB) was scattered about watching everyone. I tried to blend in, shuffling along with the civilian crowd. Bumping shoulders with the troops was inevitable. I began to notice most of those in plain grey uniforms, were my age or younger, and those with color on the shoulders were older. Most of the conversations I over heard, seemed to indicate they were headed for a training base not far away. That gave me an odd feeling in the stomach.

The mass of people moving about, pushed me around like sheep scurrying across the field to get away from the dog. There was no way I could stop and stand still. All I could think of was, *Damn, if I get mixed up with these guys and get conscripted while so close...*

Seeing a concrete column that divided the flow of bodies and presented a haven to stand against, I fought my way towards it.

With my back against the column, I lit a cigarette and looked around. *OK, there's a couple of doors the troopers ain't going thru, one of 'em has to lead outside.*

I started watching each of the doorways. A cluster of old women went through the one closest to me. *That's the women's room. Wait a minute... no toilet sign above the door, that has to be the exit.*

Taking a puff on the cigarette, I clenched it between my teeth and threw my bag over my shoulder. Dragging my left leg with a slight limp as I pushed defiantly through the crowd, I made my way towards the door.

Three meters from the doorway, and one step past the last of the KGB, a hand latched onto my sleeve. With the cigarette still clenched in my teeth, I spun around and hissed at its owner. "SShew gotch a prossblem?"

It was an older, decorated soldier in grey. "You're going the wrong way."

I jerked my arm loose. "I'sss dones my'ss time."

Stepping in front of me, he looked over at the KGB officer who was watching us.

I snarled at the grey uniform, "Youses keepssing me froms mes duty...as durected bys da KGBs."

Neither one flinched. Reaching inside my shirt as if I was going to pull out my orders, I added a new twist to my rouge. "Buts if you-ses wants to call mys superiors, please-ses do. Theys woulds loves to know yous names."

Calmly chewing on a toothpick, the soldier folded his arms and stared at me. Leaving my hand still hidden in my coat, I looked him in the eye, starting a game of who blinks first. Minutes later and neither of us moving, I growled, "Wells I's be late furs me trains ifs we keeps this up."

Biting hard on his toothpick, he glanced over at the KGB. The officer nodded. Wrinkling his nose, my agitator took the toothpick from his mouth and flicked it in my face.

Spitting the cigarette hanging from my lips at his feet, I snarled "Arrghs...shivers me's timbers matey an' full steams ahead."

Outside the station in the cool night air I shuddered with relief that my rouge had worked. Sucking in a deep breath trying to relax, I barely had enough time to exhale when a wave of people came out the door pushing me along with them. Not sure what to do, I stayed with the crowd hoping they were headed for the train station.

A few blocks from the bus terminal, the herd crossed over to the other side of the street and walked into a red-brick building that didn't look like much of a train station. This time, without hesitation, I shoved my way towards the front of the line while keeping an eye on the state security officers wondering about.

The line moved along fairly quickly. Looking up at the clock hanging from the ceiling as I walked away from the ticket window, there was still had an hour to kill before the scheduled departure. With nearly getting shanghai-ed in the bus terminal, I pondered on whether to hide in a corner, or keep hanging close to the crowd. Spotting a space along the outer wall where it looked safe and out of the way, I headed for it. Pausing at the restrooms entrance, pandering the idea that might be a safer place to hide, I could hear yelling going on inside. The men's door flew open, slamming against the wall. Two security officers came out dragging a young man into the lobby with his pants still down around his knees. *Damn, so much for that. Sitting with the crowd is it.*

Wading into the middle of the metal chairs, I sat facing the entrance doors with my back to several Air Force officers two rows behind me. Shoving my bag under my legs and my toes resting on the seat of the chair in front of me, I lit a cigarette trying to get comfortable. *Damn commies, they don't make anything comfortable.* I stretched out more, folding my hands behind my neck.

Not being able to do much, I leaned back a little further and caught part of the officers' conversation about some airplane test. It was just getting interesting when a well-endowed woman in a fur coat and mini-skirt came waltzing into the lobby off the street. My feet hit the floor with a loud thud. "Wowza."

Watching her disappear out onto the platforms, a creepy feeling roused me into sitting up straight. Casually turning around, I glanced in the officers' direction. The four of them were no longer facing the platform doorway, but were staring at me.

Raising an eyebrow, I glared back.

The highest ranking officer spoke up. "Aren't you in the wrong station?"

"Naw," I shrugged.

The youngest of the junior officers jumped to his feet and pointed towards the door. "Conscripts are to use the bus."

Suddenly my nose began twitch with his words. Taking one last draw from my cigarette, I blew the smoke in their direction. "Done my time." Then crushing the ember between my fingers, I flicked the butt in his direction and snorted, "Afghanistan," as it landed on the floor next to his feet.

"No doubt cleaning shit holes," he sneered at me.

Pursing my lips while running my tongue around the front of my teeth, I tried to think of a good comeback. The only thing coming to mind was Stefon's comment about Quartermasters being the eyes of the intelligence sector and that everyone detested them.

With my gaze focused on the senior officer, I slowly grinned, "Nope...just living in them and listening for the Quartermaster."

The look on his face told me I scored. Fingering my mustache, I stared at the group. "And to think," putting a sarcastic emphasis to my words, I waved my hand around, "how is it, I am in the luxury of a train station, hearing about how the new Mig can handle five G's and fly faster than one thousand kilometers per hour. If I remember rightly..." I made an obvious glance towards the closest KGB agent, "that kind of information is a state secret, yes?"

The senior officer slowly blinked, then lowered his eyes. Reaching into his jacket, he brandished a pack of cigarettes. "Would you care for a smoke?"

It was a premium brand. I smiled and nodded.

"Alex," he held the pack out to the junior officer.

"Yes, Major." Alex took the pack and got up. Shaking one halfway out, he held the pack in front of me. Getting cockier, I snatched the package from his hand. "Why thank you, comrade." Slipping them in my shirt pocket, I smiled, "I will speak highly of you to my superiors."

"Please do. And so I may be prepared, what are their names?"

My heart leaped into overdrive. Evidently getting too cocky for my own good, I needed a distraction. Pulling out my lighter, I flicked its lid open...closed...open...closed, while studying each of the soldiers' uniforms.

Alex snapped his fingers in my face. "Answer the Major."

The noise from his fingers made things click. "It doesn't matter what their names are. What matters is...I know yours, Major Gorky. And that of your co-conspirators... Alex, Gleb, Nicoli. Your insignia tells me what you do. And by sitting in this station, it tells me you are assigned to the air base at the end of these tracks." Scratching the end of my nose with my finger while I nodded, I then winked at him. "Shouldn't be hard to find you."

The station's loudspeaker blared out that the train to Vanino was ready for boarding, muting the Major's reply. In the silence that followed, he stared at me with steely black eyes for a moment, then got to his feet. "I don't know who you think you are...but this isn't over."

Opening my mouth and raking my tongue across my teeth, I shook my head uncaring at his comment.

"Alex..." the Major pointed to the younger man's briefcase as he grabbed his own and headed towards the platform. The others scrambled from their chairs following him out the door.

After they disappeared, I realized the adrenaline rush from the confrontation was more than I'd ever gotten from smuggling drugs for Meyer. Or even being a messenger for the godfather. Rising to my feet, my hands trembled so bad I could barely gather my things. With a shit-eating grin, I slowly sauntered out onto the platform and got on the train.

My egotistical smugness soon left me as I walked through the train looking a place to sit. Everyone stopped talking, and no one smiled, they just stared with a blank face at me passing by.

Trudging through several cars, it was obvious that comfort was not in the designer's mind when these things were built. Steel benches, with no padding, facing each other. Heaters at both ends of the cars and private lavatories with paper thin walls. Everything about it screamed 'utility,' and not the plush Euro commuter I was hoping for. Finding an empty bench, I threw my bag down and sat on it. I tried closing my eyes, but all I could see was the cattle-cars that had carried me to the Irkutsk gulags.

* * *

The train pulled into the Vanino station just before dusk. Cautiously getting off in an effort to avoid the Major and his companions, I hung back on the platform letting the crowd thin down before going through the station.

My nostrils, stinging from an odor carried by the breeze that I'd never smelled before, as I walked around in circles in the middle of an empty street. There was nothing. No street signs, no lighthouse on a hill, no sounds of a harbor. There wasn't even a porch light left on. I beginning to wonder if I had gotten off in the right town.

Hearing an engine start, I squinted through the darkness and spotted two cars parked at the far end of the station. I headed in their direction. Getting close, their inside lights showed both had someone behind the wheel, like they were possibly for hire. Stefon warned me to be careful about black market cabs, that they might take you for a long ride to nowhere. Dwelling on the options as I approached the cars; a nice shiny Mercedes, the other, a small drab-green Lada. I opened the back door of the Mercedes to throw my bag in. Hearing laughter right behind me, I turned in time for a middle-aged couple wearing furs, to push past me and climb in. Dropping my bag on the ground, I snapped, "Hey, what the—"

Ignoring me, the man tapped the driver's shoulder calling him by name, and told him to take them home. Seeing it was a lost cause, I closed the door and picked up my bag.

The beat up rusty Lada was now the only choice. Opening its front passenger door, I leaned in and asked, "How much to take me to Pier three?"

The driver didn't take his eyes off the newspaper in his hands. "Ten rubles to go to base."

Tapping on the roof of the car, I cleared my throat. "That's not what I asked. I want to go to a trawler at Pier Three."

He folded his paper. "Thirty rubles."

"That's pretty steep, ain't it?"

He opened the newspaper back up.

"Fine. You win."

My door had barely clicked shut before we sped off into the twilight. Even with no other traffic on the road, he drove as if we were in the Le Mans, and Andretti was trying to pass him. Flying up to the gateway of the pier and slamming on the brakes, we slid to a stop in the middle of the pier's entrance. As the dust settled, he turned on a small dash-mounted light and held out his right hand while keeping his left out of sight.

Looking around, all I could see in the dim light of the street lamp illuminating the pier's entrance was a rusty freighter and piles of coal. Rolling down my window, I asked, "Where's the trawler?"

Switching on the dome light, he held his hand a little closer to me. "At the end of the pier. This is as far as I go."

Not about to get out of the car until I saw the trawler. And, not knowing if this was even the right pier, I pulled three twenty ruble notes from my pocket. "I'll give you fifty to—"

He snatched the money from my hand and punched the pedal to the floor. We shot along the dimly lit dock past a half-dozen freighters and several pieces of loading equipment haphazardly parked about the pier. Skidding to a stop again, he pointed at the last ship. A trawler.

Opening the door, I put a foot on the ground. *Wait, I need to go shopping for clothes tomorrow, and I'll need a ride...*

I pulled the last one of Zarkhov's watches from my pocket. "I need to go in town tomorrow. Will this guarantee me you'll be here at ten o'clock in the morning?"

He took the watch and twisted the stem. "I'll be here at ten." Slipping it in his pocket, he placed both hands on the wheel and looked at me. "If you're not, I'm gone."

"Agreed, ten it is."

Stretching as I got out, I glanced over towards the mountains of acrid foul smelling rock waiting to be loaded on the freighters, *Oh, yeah, my change.*

The driver didn't wait, with the door still open he took off making a hard U-turn, letting the door swung shut by itself. Taking out a cigarette, I watched his tail-lights disappear into the darkness leaving me alone at the bottom of the gangway. "So much for chatting with the cabbie while he makes your change. Now...I wonder what kind of fishing tub parks next to a heap of coal, instead of closer to town with the other fishermen?"

The light illuminating the gangway was so dim, it barely lit the first few steps. Carefully climbing to the top, I looked around for a welcome mat. D*amn, no rag on the floor. So much for making a fancy entrance.*

Leaning over the railing and glancing up and down the side of the ship, there was no visible light coming out of any windows. In the dark, the tub looked abandoned. "*Man, did I just get screwed or what?*"

Stumbling along the deck in the dark, I came across another flight of stairs going up, towards what had to be the wheelhouse. I stepped through the door at the top. A lone crewman was barely visible, illuminated by the equipment lights as he talked on the radio-phone.

"Sorry to interrupt, but I'm new here. Where can I find the captain?"

Turning his back to me he, whispered into the phone and then placed it in its cradle. With a smug look on his face, he stood up, and then took off hurriedly guiding me through the inside passages to the dining facilities. Entering into the room I could feel all dozen-plus pairs of eyes follow me to the Captain's table.

"Kezel," the Captain smiled, motioning me to sit. "I was not expecting you for another three days."

"I came early to familiarize myself with the ship." I dropped my bag on the floor and sat down. "Oh...and to purchase what I need before we sail."

His smile faded. "I wanted someone who's motivated, but eagerness can cause problems. I don't want any problems. You understand?"

"Yes, sir."

"Good. Mister Khan here," he pointed to the other person sitting at the table, "will take you in town tomorrow to purchase the necessary items. If have you any questions, ask him."

"Yes, sir."

Placing his cutlery carefully on the sides of his plate, the Captain rubbed his thumbs and fingers together as he talked to me. "After you get yourself something to eat, Mister Khan will assign you a bunk."

Eager to satisfy him, I stood at attention. "Yes, sir."

Taking a sip of his coffee, he ignored me. Then setting the cup down, he wiped his mouth with a napkin, picked up his fork and resumed eating like I wasn't even there.

Nodding to myself, I took my bag and dropped it in a chair at an empty table then headed towards the food. Walking the chow line with a tray full of potatoes, bread, and onion soup, I eyed the mystery meat with caution before taking some.

Setting my tray on the table, I sat with my back to the wall facing the others in the room. About ten of them whom to be Russians, three seemed to be Kazaks or Uzbeks, and the other two I guessed to be Mongolians. The last one held my attention for the longest time as I tried to figure him out. He looked Chinese, yet he sat a full two heads higher than anyone else. Chewing on a piece of bread crust, I began to imagine how difficult it must be for him to get around the ship. So far, every door I had been through was clearly no more than six foot. The thought of banging my head on those iron door frames gave me a headache.

Mister Khan came over and stood in front of me as I picked at the food on my plate. Waiting for him to speak, I stared back, profiling him. He looked like he could have been an American Eskimo from a picture postcard.

After a few minutes, it was obvious he wasn't going to talk. Drinking the last of my water, I exhaled loudly as I glanced down at what was left on my plate. "Oh-Kay. If you say so." Standing up, I shoved the rest of the bread in my coat pocket and reached over, picking up my bag.

He didn't move.

"What?"

Pointing at my tray, then at the rack of dirty trays by the kitchen door, he looked at me.

Busing the tray, I grabbed my bag and followed the stout captain's mate into the hallway. Going down several flights of stairs and through a maze of walkways we came to a dozen door-less closets, each one had three berths stacked in it. Mister Khan stopped at the one with *#23* painted above it. He held out his hand, "You have your choice. Stow your gear in the locker at the end of the bunk, then follow me."

I tossed my bag under the bottom bunk and stood there with a grin on my face. Raising an eyebrow, he turned continuing through the corridors. Every hallway we walked through looked identical. In an effort to make sense of the maze, I stopped at one of the corners. "Where are we?"

He waved an arm. "We don't have time, let's go."

Arriving at the ship's laundry and taking a key from his hip pocket, he opened a door to a storage closet and stepped in. A pillow flew out in my direction, shortly followed by two blankets. With a sheet in hand, he stepped out and locked the door. Placing the linen on top of the wad of blankets in my arms, he snapped, "Breakfast is at six. So I suggest you get settled."

Khan disappeared down the hallway as I tried pulling the corner of a blanket from underneath my foot. Following the corridor in the direction he went, there wasn't a trace of him in the next hallway. "Khan...Khan...hey Khan." No answer. "Damn it. Ennie, meenie, minnie, mo, which way'd he go... Ummm, that way."

Guessing at retracing our steps the best I could, I made several detours in search of a bathroom. Instead of the toilet, I found part of the processing line and several dead ends with locked doors. Finding a door unlocked, I opened it. Stepping through and out onto the deck, with no one in sight and unable to hold it anymore, I dropped the bedding and danced over to the side of the ship barely making it.

Staring out across the bay at the few lights in the darkness until I finished, I zipped up and lit a cigarette. "What a deal. Either everyone is taught real well or somebody must run around and turn off the lights."

Gathering my bedding, I stepped into the corridor and left a black mark next to the door handle from the ash of my cigarette as I pulled it shut. "Oooh, not a bad idea. Mark each direction as I go and then I'll know if I'm going in circles."

Stumbling across another crewman in his bunk reading, I asked, "Does this tub have more than one bathroom?"

Tapping the wall behind his bunk, he looked at me confused, "Of course, the bunks surround them on all four walls."

CHAPTER THIRTEEN

The next morning, dragging my feet, I showed up around 6:20 to the dining room. I hoped no one would be in the chow line. Instead, I found the crew still lined up. Taking my place at the back, I mumbled out loud, "What's the problem? Everyone should've eaten by now."

The few that heard me gave me a cynical glance. Leaning against the wall, I lit a cigarette. The line hadn't moved one step by the time I finished with my smoke. Stepping over to an ashtray on a table, I could see food sitting out on the serving table. But no one was there to dish it up, nor, was the crew helping themselves.

Agitated with everyone's reluctance, I snubbed out the cigarette and marched down the line. Familiar with serving in a mess hall, I picked up the ladle stuck in a pan of what looked like watery oatmeal and the two-prong fork laying on a tray full of cut meat. I snarled at the first person in line. "You wanna eat or jack your jaw?"

Startled, he held out his tray. I slopped a ladle full of the slurry into his bowl then threw a slab of what looked like pork fat with very little meat attached to it on his plate. He didn't move. "What the fuck you waiting for?"

The crewman silently pointed toward the tray of bread sitting down the line.

"Do I look like your mother, maggot." I shoved the ladle into the gruel. "Get it yourself or go without. Now move."

After serving the next couple of crewmen, Mister Khan, patiently waiting his place in line, stepped up with two bowls and plates on his tray. Shaking my head, I tapped the rims of both bowls with the ladle. "Really?"

"Captain's."

"Right." I dipped a larger portion in one bowl, then placed the biggest, meatiest piece of pork on one of the plates.

The cook came out carrying a pan of fried diced potatoes. He watched me as I shoved the ladle into the pot and filled Khan's second bowl. "What are you doing?"

"The Captain's hungry." Glancing at the cook, I grinned, "And it looked like you needed help, so I'm helping."

Dropping the pan of potatoes between the pork and the bread, he grunted and shook his head as he walked away.

"Got anything to serve 'em with?"

He pulled a long handle serving spoon from his waistband and tossed it on top of the spuds. "One scoop."

"Ain't you gunna—"

Disappearing back into the kitchen, he ignored me. My stomach grumbled as I shoved the spoon into the spuds, leaving the handle sticking straight up. Popping one of the cubes in my mouth, I looked at Mister Khan still standing in front of me. "What?"

He pointed at the potatoes.

Hammering the ladle on the rim of pot of the gruel, I raised my voice,"Listen up people, do I look like your mother? If you want something, get it yourself. And you heard the man, one scoop...or you'll being wearin' your breakfast."

When the last person went through the line, I dished myself a plate and went to an empty table. Alone, I began to profile everyone in the room one more time. This time, with the intention to determine who I should get to know and who I should avoid. Once at sea, a slip of the tongue could mean the brig, or maybe even getting tossed over board in the dark.

Engrossed in my thoughts, I didn't see the Captain come into the dining room and stop in front of me. Tapping the table with his fingertips while momentarily staring around the room, I looked up at him. He crossed his arms. "I told you, I don't like problem makers. You decided to do someone else's work without using the normal protocol to do so."

My jaw dropped and I sat up straight. I couldn't believe he was chewing me out for helping. "Hey, if I was a little grumpy with some of the guys, then—"

His glare nearly burned holes through me.

"Sorry, sir."

"The second cook didn't show up as scheduled, yesterday." The Captain glanced over to the entrance of the kitchen. "And because of that, when you return from town with Mister Khan, you are to report to the kitchen."

The spoon I was holding, slipped out of my hand. "But, you hired me to be an electrician's mate."

Speaking through clenched teeth, he rapped his knuckles on the table in unison with his words. "It's...my...ship."

"Yes, sir."

Biting his lip, he nodded twice, then smoothed his coat and motioned to Khan standing in the doorway.

Khan came over. "Let's go."

I chomped down on a piece of bread as I wishfully looked at my unfinished breakfast. "Stores don't open for another two hours."

Taking a sip from his cup, he set it on the table. "It's a long walk to the end of the pier to get a cab."

With a smirk on my face, I stabbed at a piece of meat on my plate. "Already have one scheduled to show up at ten."

"What's the name?"

"Dunno..." I swallowed the bite in my mouth. "It was a green Lada. The driver was about thirty-five, jet black hair." I picked up my cup and sat back. "I think he wore a necklace with a single tooth or claw."

Khan nodded, "Gangway at eight."

"Why so early?"

Watching as he turned, not answering me, and walked over to a few of his friends, shook my head, *Not one pleasant person on board to talk with. This is definitely going to be one suck ass cruise.*

Arriving at the top of the gangway, seconds before Khan, he silently walked right by me and down the stairs. The green Lada pulled up and stopped at the bottom just as his foot touched the dock. Opening the front door he climbed in. Sighing at the thought of sitting in the small backseat, I opened the door and struggled to get in.

Once again, the driver took off like a rocket before I could close the door. And, like the night before, he never said a word as he drove straight into town to a boot shop.

Crawling out of the car, I followed Khan into the small shop. He went straight for the rubber boots on the far side and waited, having not been in a store for years, had to stop just inside the door and gaze at the empty shelves. Looking at their sparse inventory, I despairingly, walked from boot to boot of the twenty-odd single items on display between us.

Khan stood patiently, arms folded in front of his chest, watching me.

Getting to the six rubber boots on the wall next to Khan, I flicked one with my finger. "Damn, not much of a selection." Glancing at the clerk standing in the doorway to the backroom, a single sealskin boot hanging on the wall caught my eye. "Woo, what's that?" I grabbed it half-expecting Khan to give me some reason as to why it would be a bad choice.

He remained expressionless.

I held the boot up to his face. "This is what I want."

He didn't flinch as he asked, "What size?"

His acceptance caught me off guard. "Uh, uh, forty-four."

Khan nodded to the clerk. The rough looking shopkeeper reached into the backroom and grabbed a pair of plain rubber boots. He looked at them, raised his eyebrows, then came over and thrust them against my chest.

I grabbed the boots. "These aren't seal."

"They'll work." Khan said as he walked to the checkout counter and handed the cashier some money. "Come on."

Holding out the cheap flimsy pieces of rubber to the cashier as I walked by the counter, "They're not—"

She waved me away and turned her back to me.

Getting the impression it was fruitless to expect any kind of service, I walked out and climbed into the backseat of the taxi.

Looking at the quality of the boots as we took off, I mumbled, "I guess what I had heard while living in Germany is true. The norm in the Soviet Union is, you are lucky if you got two selections; Either you buy the one item on the shelf, or you bought nothing at all."

The driver looked at me in his mirror. "How many choices did you get in Germany?"

"Three," I grinned. "You either bought the left one; the right one; or the pair."

At the next shop, walking in, I saw a pair of Western style jeans hanging on the wall behind the clerk. Reaching into my pocket and pulling out a handful of money, I pointed at them. "I don't care what brand they are. I want those jeans on the wall."

The clerk ignoring my request, grabbed the pair of one-size-fits-all brown canvas pants from Khan's hands as he came over. She held them out, looked at me, then nodded in approval as she tossed them over my shoulder. I stared at Khan. "If I'm paying for them, shouldn't I get what I want."

"OK." Snatching the money from my hand, he counted out the price of the canvas pants and handed it to the clerk. "He'll take them." Stuffing the remainder of the cash in my shirt pocket he walked towards the door. "Come on, the taxi's waiting"

Pulling up in front of another store, I jumped out and ran into the shop ahead of Khan. From the door, I could pretty much see their entire line of inventory. The first mate brushed past me and walked over to a waterproof peacoat. He put his hand on it. Looking at me, he cocked his head.

"What are you waiting for?" I snapped as I pulled the money from my pocket. "Just bring the damn thing here."

Without waiting for him, I slapped the money on the counter and walked out to the cab. He seemed to be enjoying himself as he opened his door and threw the coat over the seat at me.

"Now that we're done, what's next? Wine? Women?"

He glanced at the driver, "Sure."

The taxi took us back to the ship at full speed. My shopping guide got out muttering, "Pay the driver." Then disappeared up the gangway.

The driver, watching me in the mirror as I fumbled with the door, announced, "Thirty-five rubles."

I tossed the boots out on the ground. "That's a hell of a lot less than what I gave you yesterday, plus a watch. Why don't we call it even?"

Taking a gun from beneath his coat, he laid it on the seat.

"That's what I thought." I pulled out what was left of the cash in my pocket; a fifty ruble note, plus a few coins. "Oh well. Keep the change," I handed it to him, "I can't spend it where I'm going."

This time, he waited for me to get everything out and close the door before rocketing off.

While putting my new clothing away, the Captain sent word for me through one of the deck hands. His office, behind the wheelhouse, was small, but plush compared to the rest of the ship. Out of habit, I stepped in taking a military stance of parade rest. "You wanted to see me, sir?"

Motioning for me to sit, he leaned back in his chair. "It looks like our second cook was paid a visit by the secret police two days ago. And no one has seen him since."

"I don't know him," I shook my head. "Never met him."

"I know when I talked with you this morning, it was to be only for a few days." He leaned foreword picking up his pen. "But as circumstances go, I need you to take his place."

It was difficult masking my disappointment, knowing I didn't have a choice if I wanted to stay on board. I protested anyway. "That's not what I signed up for, sir. I wanted to be the electrician's mate."

He sat there, pen in hand, with his usual tight-lipped gaze. His steely, cold brown eyes were hard to look at. Diverting mine to the floor, I caved. "Yes sir. I understand."

"Good. We'll be making our first rendezvous with a tender about two weeks after we leave port. They'll be bringing us another cook to replace you."

Not sure what he meant by that, I looked at him. His steeliness eased and he had an ever-so-slight of a smile as he spoke. "If you don't give me anymore problems, you'll get to be the mate then."

"Yes, sir. You can count on me."

"I hope so." Tossing his pen on the desk, he began tapping his fingertips together. "Now, be in the dining room in one hour, there's a ship-wide mandatory orientation meeting with the Political Officer. After that, go straight into the kitchen and report to Nicholas."

"Yes, sir." I got to my feet and gave him a sloppy salute as I turned to leave. His mentioning of a political officer on board, gave me the shivers as I walked out.

* * *

Ten minutes into the orientation and I had the impression I was on nothing more than a draconian slave ship. With the state, its master, and not the Captain. The political officer railed on about quotas, as if that was all that mattered. "It doesn't matter if you hate your job, or those around you, that is a moot point. Production, is the issue. And reaching our mandated goal is to be your sole focus. Even if it means giving your life for the motherland. To not achieve our goal..." his voice reaching a crescendo as he paused, he then hammered his fist on the podium, "will bring shame on the Fishing Council."

Losing interest in his preaching real fast, I began looking around at all the new faces I hadn't seen come through the chow line earlier in the morning. It looked like there were about thirty-five new people. Almost half of them women. Sizing up the women with curiosity, many of them were fairly stout. Snickering I thought, *Wonder if I would get my head ripped off if I struck up a conversation with one.* Suddenly the lights went out and a projector started. I whispered under my breath,"We get movies on this cruise, yes."

My revelry shattered as the boorish black-and-white documentary showed how the ship scooped up the fish with nets and then processes them. All for the glory of the state. The next film, claiming America was out to destroy the Soviet's way of life, with greed, over-indulgence, and individualism. BUT, if we reached our production goal, we could prevent that from happening.

By the end of the movies I had a bitter taste in my mouth. Their anti-American propaganda started to seem logical, after looking at how I ended up in the USSR. Yet, what I saw of the Soviet people, went against the American propaganda drilled into me as a citizen and soldier.—That the Soviets were America's mortal enemies. And they were nothing but, godless minions who hated Capitalism—

The political officer's rhetoric played with my logic. He railed on and on, how the motherland loved me and would take care of me no matter what, reinforcing the bitter memories of my own country stabbing me in the back. Just so a wealthy businessman could go home to his wife. My head, throbbing in pain, and my knuckles aching from my grip on the drinking glass in my hand. I tried rubbing my forehead with the glass to ease the pain. *Thirty-eight months in godforsaken Siberia and who knows how long I'll be on this stinking slave ship. All because of a political fuck-up.*

The lights clicked on, startling me. I slammed the glass down on the table, breaking it.

Staring at the shards of glass, I could feel everyone's eyes were on me. The political officer's disapproval showed on his face. Embarrassed, I commenced picking up the pieces. "Sorry, slipped out of my hands."

"What's your name?" He growled, as he slid his finger down the paper on his clipboard. "Everyone was to check in with me when they come on board."

Trying to stuff my embarrassment, I walked over to the trashcan to dispose of the glass. "It's Kez—"

"Mister Polevsky...in...my...office." The Captain stood in the doorway with his hands on his hips, glaring at the political officer.

Ignoring the Captain's command, Polevsky looked at me and repeated, "What is your name!"

"Polevsky! Now!"

Gritting his teeth, Polevsky rolled his fingers into a fist popping several of his knuckles.

Seeing that Polevsky was struggling with the Captain's command, while he stood there with his eyes burning holes through me. I stared back pointing my finger towards the Captain and grinned.

"We're not finished," he snarled as he grabbed his notes and left.

The entire assembly didn't move until Polevsky was out the door. Then in unison, everyone turned, looking at me.

Raising my hand, I waved, "Hi, I'm your new cook."

CHAPTER FOURTEEN

On the first day of working in the kitchen, Nicolas mentioned Polevsky rarely came into the mess hall to eat cause no one would sit with him. Then after he said the Political Officer had a reputation for destroying anyone around him, in his quest for power. I came to the conclusion the Captain buried me in the galley in an effort to save me from myself. That made me feel safe.

Until later in the day when the he did show up and spotted me. I could see the intense anger in his eyes as he stood in line. When it was his turn to be served, he reached over the serving table in an attempt to grab me. Out of instinct, I brought my arm up in defense. In doing so, I flicked a ladle of onion soup on his shirt.

Dropping his tray and jerking the steaming hot shirt away from his body, he screeched, "Oh, your ass is—"

Nicolas, hearing the commotion, came around the corner carrying a small loaf of bread in his hand. Pushing me out of his way, he began wiping Polevsky's shirt with it. "Calm down Polevsky, before you have a stroke. You know this ship can't run without you."

Stepping back and brushing at the mess now stuck to his shirt, he snarled, "Get me another bowl."

Nicolas shrugged and held up his hands. "Sorry, comrade. Per your instructions, we only have enough rations for one serving each." Then pointing at tray on the floor, he gave him a glum look. "You shouldn't have dropped your tray. Now move along, I have a quota to feed."

Waiting for him to leave, Nicolas handed me the ladle and whispered, "You'll be safe as long as you stay in the kitchen with me."

After dinner, on my way to the bathroom, Polevsky spotted me in the hallway. As soon as he saw me he yelled, "hey you." Running through the maze of corridors to keep away from him, it quickly became a game of hide and seek. Out of desperation, I headed for the Captain's office. Pushing his door open, I huffed, "Polevsky, sir."

Rising to his feet, he came around his desk and looked in the hallway. "OK, I'll take care of him." Pulling me in, he closed the door. "In the mean time, get back to the galley and stay there for the next two—"

A fist hammering on the door cut him short. Pushing me behind the door, the Captain opened it. "Ahh, Polevsky. Just the person I was looking for." Stepping out into the hallway, he grabbed the PO's arm. "I need your help on the bridge."

"But sir, the man in your—"

"Nonsense, there's no one in there but me. Now about the bridge."

* * *

As the Captain said, two weeks into our voyage, a re-supply ship showed up off our port side. Rough seas prevented the transferring of goods for two days. Then when the water finally calmed down enough, cables were strung between ships and the crew began transferring cargo. Through a window in the kitchen I could see a woman wearing a heavy black coat with a white scarf tied tight over her hair, standing next to the railing on the other ship. She stood waiting for over an hour before climbing into a sling to make the transfer. Watching her wild ride caused by the up and down motion of the ships, I stopped cutting vegetables and laughed, "Hey, Nicolas. Come look at this."

He came over to the window just in time to see her slap away an offer of help from the deck hands as she fought to get free of the tangled safety rope. "Son of a bitch." Nicolas growled, turning away. "Get back to work."

Half-hour later, the heavy-set woman brushed past me as she walked into the center of the galley. Putting down the can opener and wiping my hands, I offered her my hand. Slapping it aside, she got in my face. "What's your name?"

I threw my shoulders back, "Kezel Romanoff, at your service. And what be yours?"

She spun around glaring at Nicolas kneading dough at another table. "I don't work with no damn Tsarist."

Confused at who she was referring to, I glanced at Nicolas, then remembered my new last name sounded the same as that of the disposed Russian Emperor.

With a snarky smirk on my face, I walked past her to the steam kettles. She watched my every move as I turned on the water. Winking at her, I blew her a kiss. She stood sneering at me with her arms folded across her chest.

Nicolas had a rule, —Never leave the kettle while the water was running—. Figuring that during the ten minutes it would take to fill the kettle, she would relax and introduce herself to Nicolas. She remained steadfast, like a statue with its arms folded, glaring at me throughout the entire time.

Shutting off the water, I couldn't resist anymore. Squinting at her and snapping my fingers, I clicked my heels on the floor while dancing in place. "I'm a gypsy, not a Russian." Gyrating my hips, I danced towards her. "Do you want me to read your tea leaves?"

She wrinkled her nose and sneered even harder.

Enjoying the antagonism even more, I sidled up beside her and bumped her with my hip. "Or do you want me to go with you to your boudoir so to satisfy your desires?"

She spat at me and stomped out of the kitchen.

Nicolas threw his cigarette into the sink. "You sure have a way of introducing yourself. And...that probably wasn't the smartest thing to do."

"Why? What could go wrong?"

"With her...the odds are pretty good something will."

Returning, she hesitated briefly in the doorway then marched up to Nicolas, straightened her clothes, and asked, "What do you want me to do, Comrade?"

I stopped the potato peeling machine so I could hear what he had to say, hoping he'd tell her to finish peeling the spuds.

At first, he didn't say anything and just let her stand there. Glancing over at him as I hoisted a bag of potatoes, he winked at me. "Apologize to Kezel over there."

From across the kitchen I could see the hair on the back of her neck rise. "The Captain says you are the boss and to do what you say." Rolling her fingers into a fist and popping several of her knuckles, she raised her voice, "What would you like me to do, Comrade."

Nicolas stopped rolling little balls of dough and leaned toward her. "Apologize to the damn gypsy for having to do your job."

From the look on her face, I thought she was going to explode. Her face turned beet red and the muscles in her jaw twitched. Wiping my hands, I pulled out a cigarette and lit it.

She pointed at me, "Put that—"

"Woman," Nicolas growled. "I said apologize first!"

She lowered her hand, then biting her lip, she intertwined the fingers of both hands below her belly and smiled, "The Captain wants to see you in his office."

With as much sarcasm as I could muster, I grinned, "Are you talking to me?"

"Yes," she hissed.

I looked at Nicolas.

He nodded, then went back to making little balls of dough.

Taking a deep drag from my cigarette, I glanced at her. Her squinted eyes were full of fire. "Here, this should cool you down." I flicked my cigarette at her, trying to make it into her open shirt.

She jumped and brushed at the burning sparks on her blouse. "You little—"

"Excuuuse me." I bumped her with my shoulder as I walked by. Before she could react, Nicolas snapped, "Comrade, go finish peeling the potatoes."

The Captain had left his door slightly ajar. I rapped on it with my knuckles as I pushed it open and stepped in. "You wanted to see me, sir?"

He glanced up from his desk. "Kezel, come in." Flipping the notebook in front of him closed, he motioned towards an empty chair adjacent to his desk. "Shut the door."

Reaching for the doorknob, Mister Khan startled me as he stepped in and grabbed the knob. Gulping, I slid into the chair with the impression I was about to get my ass chewed out again.

Looking very distinguished with his closely trimmed beard, the Captain leaned back in his chair and tapped his fingertips together a few times before speaking. "Mrs. Brevshevnic comes highly recommended by the Fishing Council. And, so does Mister Polevsky. Remember that."

I nodded, waiting for the ass-chewing to begin.

"I know you signed on to be the electrician's mate. But...I'm changing that," he looked me straight in the eyes killing my effort to protest. "I'm going to give you two jobs instead. Maybe that will keep you occupied enough to stay out of trouble."

Uncertain as to what he meant, I sat biting the tip of my tongue, waiting for the worst.

"Your new job is going to put you out amongst the crew, so I want that thing you wear around your neck." He held out his hand. "I don't need any of the crew doing something stupid if they were to see it."

"No way." I leaned back clutching the talisman under my shirt. "It's mine."

Mister Khan stepped beside me placing his hand on my shoulder. "You'll get it back at the end of the season. I promise."

I folded my arms over it and stared at the Captain. "Really? I was promised the mate's job. Now you—"

"You have the mate's job," he interrupted me. "And you're also to be Khan's assistant."

I sat stunned, gazing at the wall behind the Captain. *I can't believe it. Working with Khan would give me access to the bridge...and the charts. Wait a minute, the condition is only if I give up these teeth that Babushka gave me.*

Holding out his hand, the Captain wiggled his fingers. "For your own protection."

With a deep sigh, I untied the knot in the leather string around my neck and placed the talisman in his hand. Looking at the tiger's teeth, he rubbed them with his thumb and nodded, "Their power is impressive." Taking a breath, he slipped the necklace into an envelope and wrote my name on the front. After sealing it, he held the package out. "Put it in the safe Mister Khan."

As the first mate leaned over placing the envelope into the safe, he held his lips close to it and whispered, "Forgive me, brother."

Picking up his pen, the Captain leaned forward with his elbows on the desk, staring at me. "You are not to talk to Polevsky under any circumstances. If he happens to question you about anything, you are to tell him to come see me, and then keep your mouth shut. Do you understand?"

The seriousness in his voice was somewhat smothering. "Yes sir," I nodded.

His face lightened up. "Good." Laying his pen down, he clasped his hands together. "Your main focus will be to keep that drunken son-of-a-bitch electrician from getting hurt or putting other people's lives in danger." Glancing over at Khan, then back at me, "We don't need another deadly incident."

I looked at Khan, then at the Captain. Shaking my head I asked, "Why don't you fire him?"

The Captain bit his tongue as he clicked the pen open and closed several times.

Khan whispered, "Ivan is Captain's brother."

Familiar with loyalty to one another in the military regardless if you liked your team mates or not, but I could sense there was something different; family loyalty. Opening my mouth to say, 'so what, get rid of him,' the sudden remembrance of the pain endured by those in prison when a family member turned them in to the secret police. Instead, I offered, "I understand, sir."

Resuming his composure, he continued, "On days when he's too drunk to work safely, you are to send for me or Khan. Then stay with him until we get there. Understand?"

"Yes, sir."

"Good. Don't disappoint me." He picked up a folded piece of paper from his desk and held it out. "Go find Ivan and give him this."

With mixed feelings about the added responsibility, I took the paper. "Yes, sir."

* * *

It didn't take long carrying tools for the grumpy, hung-over maintenance man, before I began feeling like nothing more than a glorified babysitter. He was difficult to be around and had a tendency to throw tools before he had a drink. When I asked how the machine worked, he growled something about job security and sent me after a tool he had left at the other end of the ship. I searched for half an hour and never found it. Upon returning and telling him it wasn't there, he answered, "Oh well."

By the third trip of the day looking for the same tool and not finding it, I realized why the wild-goose chases. What he really wanted was a nip from a small flask of vodka hidden somewhere close by.

Returning after my fifth goose chase, Ivan was so plowed he had trouble standing. Watching him trying to work around the moving machinery gave me the willies. I called Mister Khan. Showing up, Khan convinced Ivan to go with him to look at another project. As they walked away, Khan said to me over his shoulder, "Close up those connection boxes, put his tools away and then go grease or oil the equipment. Just remember; stay away from Polevsky."

It was difficult not to interact with the rest of the crew while greasing the equipment they were using. And it wasn't hard to see we were headed eastward. Even Polevsky said we would be following the salmon in the Pacific current. Yet down to the man they all acted as if they didn't trust me and avoided my questions about our following the fish. Several of them quickly changed the topic, bitching about the nets coming back filled to only one third of capacity.

Even though I was new on board, things didn't seem right with everyone being so tight lipped.

* * *

Desperate after six weeks at sea and not having the information as to where our supposed fishing grounds were in relation to the American coastline, I decided to help Ivan loosen up a little and see what I could get out of him.

The next morning, grabbing a cup of coffee to go as I left the mess hall, I slipped into the electrical room ahead of Ivan and poured some of his hidden liquor into it. When the grumpy old man finally managed to walk in, I pointed toward the cup, "I brought you some coffee."

"Why?"

"No reason, just thought it would make your day easier."

"Neeyeaaah." Hesitating,then flopping into his chair, he grabbed the mug and waved it under his nose. Glancing at me as he took a sip, he smiled, "You may make it yet."

"You think so?" I picked up one of the manuals on the desk and started thumbing through it. "At the rate you're letting me do things, we'll be back in port for the winter before then."

"Phift."

I glanced at him. "What, we just gunna sit out here and wait for them to swim by?"

"We haven't begun chasing the fish yet. We'll go right up the American coastline after 'em. You still got time."

"Hmm, along the coastline. It'd still be nice to know how things work before we get to...where?"

"Enough of this small talk, we got a lot of work to do." Setting the empty mug on the desk next to my arm, he started rummaging through a stack of work orders. "Go get me another one. Only this time, not so much sugar."

Rising, I snatched the cup. "Maybe I'll fill it with nothing but... That might sweeten your attitude."

Tossing the cup around in my hands as I walked towards the door, Ivan yelled, "And watch out for Polevsky."

"Don't you worry about me..." I said fumbling the cup as I reached for the door, "you just be ready to work by the time I get back."

When I returned with a fresh cup, Ivan was still looking at the work orders. I set the coffee down in front of him. "I thought I told you to be ready."

Downing half the contents in one gulp, he set the cup down and shoved his chair back. "Watch it. Now, go get my tool box and let's go"

In the passageway, at the top of the stairs to the deck below, he downed the rest of the coffee, setting the cup on the floor against the wall as he started to descend. Seeing no one around, I whispered, "What's the possibility of docking at an American port?"

His laugh, barely audible at first, grew louder with each step till he was laughing so hard he stumbled and fell, sprawling onto the pile of fish net laying at the bottom. Doing what the Captain said to do when he got drunk, and since touching the slimy, foul smelling net to help him up was not in my job description, I sat on the bottom step and pulled out a cigarette. Exhaling slowly, I examined the cigarette in my hand while watching Ivan out of the corner of my eye. Each time he moved, he became tangled up even more, causing him burst out laughing.

After what seemed like an eternity, Ivan made an effort to sit up. The net was hooked around every button on his shirt, weighting him down.

Lighting another cigarette and taking a drag, I tried blowing smoke rings in his direction.

By now his bouts of laughter were quickly turning into a hushed whimpering. Three of the net crew, prepping it to be rolled up, stopped as soon as they saw who it was tangled up. Looking at Ivan, then at me, one of them asked, "What happened?"

"Nothing, he just missed the bottom step and thought it was funny." I reached for Ivan's arm. "OK, Ivan. Let's get you free."

He burst out laughing again as soon as I said that. I looked over at the net crew. "What'd I say that was so flippin' funny?"

The three of them shook their heads and didn't offer any help.

I tugged on his arm, "You ready now?"

He didn't reply.

"Ivan!" I kicked his foot, he was out cold. Looking over at the crew I shrugged, "Now what?"

One of them pointed towards the intercom box behind the stairs. Giving him the thumbs up, I went over and called for Mister Khan.

When Khan arrived, he took one look at Ivan, then went over to the net crew speaking with them in a hushed tone. Showing little enthusiasm for what ever was said, they returned to working on the net. Turning, Khan headed for the stairs, motioning me to follow him.

"What about, Ivan?"

"Leave him."

I paused on the bottom step. "What?"

"They'll take care of him," he said as he climbed the stairs. "You're needed elsewhere."

* * *

Now in our seventh week at sea, a freighter rendezvoused with us and exchanged supplies for all the frozen fish we had in the hold. Shortly after their departure, the Captain sent for me.

This time, when I stepped in his office, he left the charts out on his desk. Standing on the carpet in front of him, I waited for him to clear them away before I sat. Mister Khan, in the mean time, stepped in from the hallway and closed the door.

The Captain, leaning back in his chair, motioned, "Grab a chair and bring it closer." He tossed the pack of cigarettes from his pocket on the map. "Cigarette?"

Surprised at his sudden openness, but still having that feeling I was about to get my ass chewed out for something stupid, I humbly pulled the chair next to his desk and took one from the pack. His lighter lay on the other side of the map. I pointed to it. He nodded and picked up the ashtray beside his arm, placing it on a land mass along the map's edge.

Trying not to make it too obvious I was glancing at the chart as I reached over to pick up the lighter. I could see the ashtray sat on the Oregon and Washington coastline. Biting my tongue, I sat back in my chair.

The Captain finally broke the silence. "To make our newly imposed quota, we need to venture into the American Economic Zone. That's where the salmon concentrate before going into their rivers. And..." he gripped his pen a little tighter, "I need you to help Ivan get the sonar equipment operational before we get there."

Confused at his statement, I looked at him cocking my head. "We have a working sonar, yes?"

"Yes, but the final piece of equipment that was to have been installed while we were in port for the winter, arrived on that last transport. We need it to pinpoint and identify the fish, along with giving us the size of the school."

That didn't make sense; we could already do that. But what did I know. All I knew, was with Ivan, that getting anything done on time would be more impossible than swimming the two hundred miles to the North American coastline.

I drummed my fingers on the map wanting nothing more than to get close to shore. Sighing loudly, I looked up from the map at him. "Yes, sir. How many days do we have?"

"Four."

I almost swallowed my cigarette. "Impossible. Not with that drunk." I looked over at Khan in disbelief.

He bit his lip and raised his eyebrows in a sign to keep my mouth shut.

"Sorry, sir. I'll do whatever it takes."

"Good." The Captain opened the top drawer of his desk, pulled out a key-ring with half-dozen keys on it and tossed it on the map. "These will give you access to anyplace you need to go."

"Yes, sir, but I am just learning how the wires—"

"I don't have a choice, Kezel. The fish are following the Pacific current, which flows towards the American coast line." He sat tapping his lighter on the map. "You're the only one I have to get this job done on time."

I couldn't believe him, but I knew I was going to be the scapegoat if the project failed. And, when it did, I wouldn't care. We'd be so close to the US, I'd make my escape in one of their survival rafts. Picking up the keys, I held them in my hand judging their weight. "Is there a manual with this piece of equipment?"

Khan handed me a notebook full of handwritten notes and diagrams. Page after page were filled with cursive Russian writing. I felt faint. Fairly fluent in the spoken word, I could decipher much of the block form alphabet, but with cursive, I was totally lost. Without Ivan's help in deciphering the notes, I was definitely doomed to fail.

The Captain must have sensed my vexation. Reaching into the lower drawer of his desk he pulled out a bottle of vodka, along with a small glass. "I've watched you with Ivan." He poured a shot in the glass and slid it over next to my hand. "I wouldn't have asked you if I thought you couldn't do it. You need to trust me."

Wrinkling my nose, I let the drink sit. This was beginning to sound familiar.

First looking up at Khan standing behind me, then at me, he reached into the drawer and pulled out another glass. Khan set his coffee cup down next to the Captain's, who then filled each of the three cups half full.

The first mate picked up his cup and presented a toast. "To our success of this endeavor."

Snatching mine from the desk, I hoisted it. "To success." Still hesitant, I waited for them to swallow theirs first.

Captain raised his cup to his lips and tossed the shot down.

The vodka burned my throat as it went down. Gasping for air, I got to my feet and mustered as much of a self-assured stance as I could before blurting out, "I won't fail you, sir."

Khan opened the door for me.

Stepping from the Captain's office, my head started to swirl at hearing the first mate whisper as I stepped out, "Remember, everything floats toward their coastline."

Or, maybe it was just the vodka.

CHAPTER FIFTEEN

I didn't sleep a wink all night trying to come up with some idea for making this sonar thing work in my favor. When I finally crawled out of my rack, I still didn't have an idea. Frustrated, tired, I thumbed through the notebook while eating breakfast. It dawned on me as I shoveled the last of my food into my mouth, that the notes weren't installation instructions, but more like descriptions of junction box locations within the ship as shown in the diagrams. "That's it," I muttered tearing three pages out and shoving them in my pocket. "Now all I need is to get Ivan on board."

Filling a thermos with coffee, I stopped by one of his caches of vodka to add a little flavoring on my way to the electrical shop. At his desk with his head resting on his arms, Ivan ignored my noisy entrance.

"That's our new agenda," I said, dropping the book next to his arm.

He didn't move.

"Hey," I pulled my chair beside the desk and tapped on the notebook with my fingers before sitting. "Captain says this has priority."

He waved his hand at me. "Get me a cup of coffee."

Reaching for the carafe on the bench, I shook it. *Ahh, leftover from yesterday. That ought to perk him up.* I poured some in his cup. "Here."

Ivan sucked in a taste of the cold coffee. Gagging, he spit it out. "Get me some hot coffee I said." He shoved the cup across the desk towards me as he laid his head back down.

Wiping off the spilt coffee from the desk before pouring a fresh mouthful in his cup, I placed it out of his reach. "Look at the book and I'll give you this."

He peeked at the book through one eye. "What is it?"

"It's our new project the Captain handed me yesterday," I said as I held out the cup.

Ivan sat up and studied the first page as he took a sip of the fresh coffee. Turning to the second page, he slid his empty cup toward me. I filled it and quietly shoved it back in front of him. On the third page he stopped reading and stuck his finger in the middle of a diagram. Looking at the drawing all around his finger he began shaking his head. He then started flipping pages back and forth trying to trace a single line. Suddenly, he banged his fist on the desktop. "Damn them."

I looked up from the materials needed list I was making. "What's the problem?"

Grabbing his cup, he swirled its contents under his nose for a second before downing it. Leaning back in his chair he snarled, "The Council continually sends us plans and equipment to improve our quotas. And as usual, half the time they're missing pages."

Staying focused on my list, I wrote down, 'ladders' as I asked, "Can we still do it?"

"I think so. Fortunately, the first and last pages are here. I should be able to fill in the missing pieces."

Glancing at him over my clipboard, I watched as he stared at the first page, then flipped to the last, then back to first, then to the last again. "Damn, why did they choose that route? A child could have done better."

He flipped the notebook shut and reached for his cup. Seeing it was empty, he threw it at the workbench. Sitting there growling, he rubbed his forehead for a moment then lit a cigarette and leaned back closing his eyes. I kept my attention focused on the clipboard in my hands.

After a few puffs, he walked over to the bench and picked the cup up off the floor. His hands shaking, he struggled to pour the last of the coffee from the carafe, into it. Out my peripheral vision, I watched as he held the drink close to his nose and sniffed it. With a sour look he set it down on the bench and returned to his chair.

I snickered, tossing my clipboard and pencil on the desk. "What's the matter, doesn't taste the same as the last cup?" Lacing my fingers together behind my neck, I stretched out my legs. "That's from yesterday, I brought some fresh in this morning."

He ignored me as he picked up my notes. "What's this?"

"A list of material we'll need."

Ivan glared at me as he chucked the clipboard back on the desk. "They didn't deliver material with the equipment?"

"How the hell should I know? I was working in the galley during the last resupply." Getting up and retrieving a bottle of vodka from under the bench where I had placed it as I came in, I grinned, "Besides, it's your duty to the motherland to get this project done." Making sure he watched me pour a shot into my coffee, I held onto the bottle as I sat down, placing it on the floor between my feet.

He bit his lower lip, glaring at me through narrow slits.

I reached over and took a cigarette from his pack. Half-way through with the cigarette and tired of his staring, I poured a shot in his cup. "To the best electrician on the seven seas," I said, holding my cup up high. "I have faith in you."

He took his cup, held it at arms length for a second, then poured its contents down his throat. Gently setting the cup down, he got to his feet. "You're full of shit. Let's go to work."

* * *

The next day, when he came to the first missing page, Ivan leaned against a wall studying the note. Impatient, I fought with the idea of getting him drunk. If he were drunk, I could do what I wanted to fuck up the job and increase my chances of forcing the ship into an American port. Standing next to the railing trying to keep my balance on the rolling deck, I looked at the rising swells, whispering, "Or, I could go to my rack and let him prove what he is capable of doing. Naw, suck it up and do your job."

Mister Khan came by late in the afternoon to check on our progress. Standing next to me while watching Ivan fumble with a screwdriver as he tried turning the screws on a junction box cover, Khan whispered, "This is the longest I've seen him stand upright in the last year."

"You've got to be kidding." I shook my head at the thought. "Why do you keep him on board then? Because he's family?"

"No. He used to be the best electrician in the fleet and had been given multiple accommodations from the Fishing Council. That was... until he lost his daughter several years ago. Now, he's..."

Mister Khan's statement stung. Loosing someone you love is a bitter pill to swallow. I looked at Ivan, *Damn it Ivan, I feel for you, but fuck if I'm going to let a drunk ruin my chance to escape.*

Khan patted me on the arm and turned away. "You're doing fine. The Captain will be happy."

"Yeah, tha—" I winched, seeing Ivan slip with the screwdriver, stabbing his finger.

"Damn it." Ivan howled, shoving his finger in his mouth.

"Here," I threw him a roll of electrical tape. "I need to go pee. You need anything? Water? Coffee?"

He shook his head as he wrapped his bleeding finger with tape.

After using the latrine, I made my way to an electrical junction box on a different deck where I had found another small bottle of hooch hidden inside earlier in the week. Slipping the flask into my coat pocket, I made a bee-line to where I had left Ivan earlier.

His toolbox was there, but he wasn't. Checking around in the vicinity and still no Ivan, I placed the bottle in his toolbox and went to eat supper.

Finished with supper and Ivan still hadn't showed up in the mess hall, I glanced at my watch. *It's gunna get dark soon, I better go find him, just to keep the Captain off my back.*

It took me a good twenty minutes to meander to the ass end of the ship. Sitting down where I could overlook the nets as they were being pulled in, I lit a smoke and tried to study the diagrams I had ripped from the book. When it came time for the net full of fish to be emptied onto the deck, the birds that were following us, started swarming overhead. They'd hover up out of reach, then dive down trying to steal any morsel of fish they could. Captivated with the melee, I shoved the notes in my pocket just as bird crap hit the railing in front of me. *Ahh shit, thanks for reminding me. I better go find him.*

Making my way back to where I'd left him, Ivan wasn't there, nor was his toolbox. But he did leave the spools of wire we were pulling into the pipes. *Oooh, yeah. I don't need his help. He's always wantin' to mark every single frickin' wire. What a waste of time, I can pull it in faster without him.*

Working by myself, I got more ground covered in two hours than the whole day with him. Pulling the notes from my pocket, I looked at them, *Dang, I'm gunna have to do something soon or I'll have done too much and have screwed myself.*

Following the next section of pipe led me into the huge freezer where the processed fish was stored. In the middle of the storage bay, six meters up, the pipe ran into a junction box with twelve other pipes connected to it. "Oh yeah baby. There it is...the perfect place. There's where my ace of spades is gunna be. At the right moment, some douche bag's gunna flip a switch...and bingo...the ship's gunna screech to a halt. And when that happens...I'm overboard."

One of the forklift drivers waiting for the line to catch up, hoisted me up to the box and helped pull in the new wires from both sides of the freezer. Before closing the junction box on the ceiling, I randomly grabbed four wires hoping they weren't energized and spliced onto them with four of the six new wires I pulled in. Knowing Ivan would never check my work up there, I left the ends of the new wires on both sides of the freezer hanging out of their boxes for him to see and pulled through another fifty meters of pipe before stopping for the night.

* * *

As promised, on the morning of the fourth day, with the Captain present, Ivan turned the new sonar machine on. Its screen glowed a pale green, but lacked any indications of receiving a signal. The Captain folded his arms as he studied the screen. "Ivan, are you sure you've got everything hook up right?"

Ivan stepped back and lit a cigarette. Taking a puff, he grabbed my arm, "Kezel, crawl underneath that damn thing and make sure all the cables are connected."

Gritting my teeth, I looked at him.

"Do as I say lad."

I laid on my back and cautiously slid under the device. Tugging gently on each of the wires, I relayed, "They're all connected."

Rolling his eyes, the Captain turned toward the chart table. "Ivan, get the book and meet me in my office. Mister Khan," the Captain put a mark on the map, "follow the fish into American water. And..." he pointed at me, "you make sure every junction is securely made up. Understand?"

"Yes, sir," I snapped as he walked out of the pilothouse.

Going straight to the freezer, where all the wires had been left disconnected, I went to the port side first. There, connecting the sonar wires randomly to other wires in the box, I was fortunate nothing blew up in my hands and only created a few sparks causing me to blink. Over on the starboard side, I connected wires together without following Ivan's markings. Smug with the fact that I hadn't electrocuted myself, I took my time re-inspecting the rest of the junctions.

As I continued my inspection into the bowels of the ship, an unusual number of bells came over the ship's horn. At first, thinking it was a man-overboard signal, I ran up to the deck. Instead of seeing someone in the water, on the horizon, a ship was closing in from the east at a very high rate of speed.

As it steamed toward us, I strained to see if it was an American, or maybe a Canadian vessel. Its straight on approach hid their flag. Not until the ship was within a few football field lengths away, and stopped, could I see the stars and stripes. I hit the railing and hissed, "Yes," under my breath.

The Coast Guard cutter sat there for about five minutes, then slowly started circling our trawler in an ever tightening manner. Each time around, the features of the men at their guns became clearer. At about the length of a football field off our bow, the cutter stopped and put a small launch into the water.

Leaning over the railing, I studied the swells, trying to estimate my odds of swimming to the American's ship. *This might be my closest chance—*

A hand on my shoulder followed by a familiar voice from behind, interrupted my thoughts. "They'll just hand you back over to the KGB."

Startled, I lost my balance, falling onto the deck. Using the railing to climb to my feet, I looked at him innocently. "Ahh, Nicolas. What are you talking about?"

"I've seen that look of... *I can make it.*" He leaned backward on the railing next to me and looked up at the bridge. "Don't fool yourself."

I lit a cigarette and rested my elbows on the railing next to him, looking out over the ocean. "What do you mean? I have no intention of leaving Mother Russia."

"Uh huh, sure." He took the cigarette from my hand. "Two years ago I was on another trawler when a Latvian baled over the side and swam to the American's launch."

I lit another one for myself. "And?"

Inhaling a long drag, he turned around facing the water and slowly exhaled. Pensive, he flicked the ash from his cigarette into the water. "The Americans handed him back within the hour. Both the Latvian and the ship's captain were taken to Moscow for trial."

"Like I said, I am faithful to the Motherland. But, haven't you ever wondered what it would be like to visit one of their ports?"

"Naw. Their vodka is like piss-water from what I hear." He flicked his cigarette into the ocean. "What good would it be to go where there's no vodka, eh? Let's go before Mr. Polevsky sees you looking at the American's ship."

Back inside, resuming my work in a half-ass manner, I traced the wires into the processing room. From my perch on my ladder, I could see the machinery was turned off and the workers stood around idle in groups of twos and threes.

Finished in the processing area, I folded the ladder and headed for the next box. Needing to get by one of the groups, I asked as they made way, "How come the machine's down?"

Two of the three shook their heads and looked away, the third muttered, "The machinery is fine. As long as the Americans are on board, it has to be shut off." He put a finger to his lips, "A state secret."

I laughed thinking he was making a joke. "Ahh, yes. The Americans wanting to steal—"

Suddenly an explosion rocked the ship followed by fire bells, sending everyone to their stations. Dropping the ladder, I took off for the bridge.

Reaching the bridge, the door was thrown open by another deckhand coming out, in time for me to hear Mr. Polevsky slap his hand on the chart table demanding the Americans leave the ship. Surprised to see an armed boarding party, I had a sudden urge to rush over and yell...*I'm an American.*

Khan, seeing me standing in the doorway, turned from the confrontation and glared at me. Nodding, I slipped into a corner out of everyone's way and watched the confrontation while I questioned Nicolas' words.

Mr. Polevsky continued his shouting match with the Captain about political protocol in dealing with the boarding party. The American officer kept trying to get between them demanding in English, "What the hell's going on?" Standing there watching, I got the impression no one in the boarding party spoke Russian, and none of the bridge crew spoke English. The chaos grew into a hysterical circus with everyone yelling their demands. In an effort to help, I took several steps toward the Americans intending to translate for them.

Khan grabbed my arm. "Don't. Go find Ivan and make sure he is sober."

I glanced at the soldiers, then at Khan. "If he isn't?"

"Make him that way and..." Khan paused, straining to hear the words coming from a speaker on the other side of the pilothouse. When the speaker went silent, he shoved me towards the door. "Stay with him and keep him away from that engine fire."

Looking at the three-ring circus, then at Khan, I shook my head in disgust, mumbling, "Polevsky is such a dumb-shit. The least he could do is ask for some American cigarettes."

Starting with the top deck, I checked the life rafts, debating, before making my way to the lower deck. Then into the electrical shop, where I found him at his desk, pouring over the prints for the engine room. Without a word, I slipped into my chair and watched him.

After skimming over several pages, he spoke up. "Go get me some coffee."

"Can't do. The Captain said he needs you to stay sober."

"What's that got to do with getting me some coffee?"

"Because of what you put in it."

"Go get me some coffee."

I answered in a snarky tone, "Khan said, and I quote, do not leave him."

Ivan sat up and slammed his fist on the desk. "I don't give a damn what Khan said. If I don't find a way to get fuel to those engines, we'll be swimming back to Moscow for our trial. Now get me some damn coffee."

"The engines are on fire. How the hell is getting them fuel going to help?"

Ivan picked up the book and drew his arm back. "Now!"

Having never seen him so angry before, I jumped out of the chair, "OK, OK."

When I returned with a full thermos, he was standing in front of the filing cabinet pulling manuals out one at a time. After thumbing through it, he either threw the booklet on his desk or on the floor.

Pouring him a cup of coffee, I sat down. "What did you mean by, swim to Moscow?"

Glancing over at me he continued to paw for tidbits of information in the manuals. "The engines are dead and in thirty-six to forty hours we'll be washed up on shore. And for some reason the radio is not transmitting. If we can't contact another ship to tow—"

I cut him off. "The Americans are still on board. They'll tow us to port."

"God forbid that should happen." Walking over to the desk, he picked up his coffee. His hands shaking so bad as he tried to take a drink, he managed to spill half of the cup all over the top of the desk. I fetched one of his hidden bottles, poured a shot into his cup then took a swig for myself.

"Thank you." He carefully used two hands to take a sip. "If the Americans tow us without Moscow's approval, everyone on board will stand trial for treason." Wiping the sweat from his head with a rag, he cringed as he carried on. "With my record, I won't get a trial. It'll be straight to the camps."

The thought of prison seemed to have a more sobering effect on him than the coffee. Sitting quietly in my chair, I watched a drunk who was just another pawn in my plan of escape, wallow in self-pity. I took another swig from the bottle, capped it, then suggested, "You could always jump ship."

He glared at me through bloodshot eyes. "What? Abandon my brother...never. If I jumped, it would be like putting the gun to his head myself."

"They wouldn't execute him because of what you did," I countered, trying to convince him that to escape would be his best option.

Pointing his finger at me, he growled, "Have you ever been through one of those trials? My brother would—"

A scratchy, crumpling-paper sound came from the intercom, interrupting him. "Ivan! Kezel! To the bridge immediately."

As I stood up, I watched his face go pale. He was fearing something I didn't know about and just sat there. Waiting a few minutes, I waved my hand towards the door, "Shall we?"

Upon entering the bridge, I saw that the Americans had left, and so had Polevsky. The Captain was leaning over an opened chart of the Oregon Coast writing on a piece of paper. Handing it to Khan, he turned and faced Ivan. "Ivan, prepare the ship to be towed to port."

"But," Ivan protested.

"We don't have a choice. A storm is closing in and will push us aground before help can arrive. The Americans will assist us till our own towing vessel can get here."

"I won't. You're not going to force me, Alex." Ivan stood, fists clenched. "I'd rather drown, than go back to those camps."

The Captain, with his usual calmness, eyed his brother. The two stared at each other longer than I thought they would. Sitting down in a chair waiting for the family feud to play out, I started watching the pilot trying to ignore the commotion too.

The Captain finally broke the silence. "That could be arranged, so don't tempt me to throw you over board before we get to port. Go do what I asked."

Ivan spun on his heels and stomped out the door. Pushing myself up from the chair, I started to follow.

"Not you, Kezel. I have something else for you to do." The Captain held out a folded piece of paper. "Here is a list of what I want you to do, and it must be done in exact order, and at the exact time stated. Understand?"

Glancing at the paper, then at him, I shrugged, "Sure."

CHAPTER SIXTEEN

The growing ocean swells made it tricky to walk. Sliding my elbow along the inside passage wall as I walked, gave me some stability while reading the Captain's note. His instructions made no sense. "What the hell is this? Go to the galley first, then go to the front of the ship and wait till I hear three bells, then go to the ass end an hour later, then take a different route forward to a closet on the deck below the first location.... Damn, I can't believe he wrote this. Oh well, he's da man, an' number one says go to the galley and tell Nicolas to prepare a cold meal for seven people."

When Nicolas heard the Captain's message, he grinned and patted me on the cheek. "Thank you, my friend."

Folding my arms, I eyed him. Usually he would piss and moan about any extra work, but this time he grabbed a dishrag and started whistling as he cleaned his work table. "Now be off."

"Can I get—"

"Finish what you were told to do first...exactly how you were told. Then come back."

Standing in the doorway I read the next item out loud, "Get to the engine room by 15:30 and tell the engineer Pavel, to get pump number seven ready for operation." I looked at my watch. "Why the hell am I doing this one? I'll have to run to make it on time. He could do it faster himself over the intercom."

"Go!" Nicolas yelled.

The engine room was dead quiet, except for Pavel's voice bitching about fire retardant all over the room. Normally, with the engines running, you couldn't hear a hammer hit the metal deck. But with the silence, it was easy to follow the sound of his voice. I tapped Pavel on the back. He let out a scream, dropping the wrench in his hand. "Damn it lad. Don't ever sneak up on me like that again. Now what do you want?"

"Get ready to turn on pump seven."

"Pump seven?" He grabbed my arm. "Did you say pump seven?"

I nodded.

"It's about time." He ushered me to the door. "No time to talk, finish what you were told to do."

Pushing against the door jam to keep from being ejected out of the room, I asked, "What's pump seven do? I haven't seen it on any of the diagrams."

"It's an emergency pump." He patted me on the arm. "Go! You need to finish your work."

I snorted as I looked at my watch, "I still got two hours till the next item. So what does pump number seven do?"

"I don't have time talk. Come back in a couple of days..." Scowling, he pushed me out the door and closed it.

Pulling out the paper and looking at it, *OK, that went well. What's the next item... EM Bilge Pump 263b, located mid-ship. Once found, stand by and wait. Three bells will sound at 1800 hours, throw switch.*

Going down amongst the processing equipment while the crew took the opportunity to clean the idled machinery, I searched and searched for pump 263b's control box. After an hour of fruitless searching, I started asking people where I might find the box's location. They all gave me the same expression and shrugged their shoulders. Finally, a rough looking character with tattoos all over him, pointed towards a slicing machine, "Go look over there. There's several control switches behind the conveyor."

"Thanks, brother," I held out my hand.

He looked at my hand, snorted, and went back to his washing the equipment.

Hidden by the machine, the switch, along with several others, were mounted to a support post. *What a flippin' place to put an emergency bilge pump control switch.* I looked at my watch, *Damn, an hour still to go. May as well take a seat.*

Cramming the list in my pocket, I sat down and took a out cigarette, lighting it. Leaning against the wall and being rocked by the ship's movement, it was a struggle not to fall asleep. I pulled the list from my pocket to give me something to do. *Let's see, next item...Find Krezenskiin bunk #457, tell him Mrs. Wrojeck needs his help in dispensary securing seven cases of medication.*

"Damn," I blurted out. "I could have done that on my way here. It just don't—"

"Hey, put that out."

"What?"

"There's no smoking down here."

Peeking under the conveyor belt, the tattooed crewman was pointing a hose at me.

"Sorry, didn't know." I snubbed the cigarette out on the floor. "OK?"

He left without answering.

"Now...what's after Krezenski ? From there, the rest seems to be a double check of Ivan's work on preparing the ship to be towed..." *Oh, and a list of miscellaneous pumps to be tuned on or off. Whoa, here we go. A back up plan just in case we don't get towed by the Coast Guard.*

I looked at the list again with thoughts of destroying the emergency bilge pump switch. *Wait a minute, didn't Ivan say that we don't have enough power to run all the pumps and that we could still go down if the sea gets too rough. Naw, I don't want to be shark bait.*

Leaning sideways stretching my butt muscles, I glanced at the half-dozen pair of legs running around cleaning equipment. "Damn, this is dragging on forever."

Sitting up and reading the last line the Captain's writing, it was a bit vague. A single letter was throwing me off. If pronounced one way, it meant crane. If pronounced another way, it could mean bridge.

"Hmm...", I twisted my neck in an effort to relieve its stiffness, "Not knowing which it is, is going to pose a—"

Three bells rang out over the horn interrupting my thoughts. Clamoring to get to my feet, I threw the switch, then took off at a brisk walk to find bunk #457.

After finding Krezenskiand telling him to go help Mrs. Wrojeck, I stepped outside onto the main deck and saw the Coast Guard was trying to transfer a person ship-to-ship.

Mr. Khan came up some stairs close by.

I nodded towards the their vessel. "What's going on?"

He watched them for a moment. "Hmm, that'll be the bar pilot."

"Hey, Khan," I pointed towards the Americans, "what's that light on the other side of their ship?"

Opening the door I had just came through, he mumbled, "A channel buoy."

"How close are—" the metallic click of the door latch told me I was talking to myself. Yanking the door open, I ran after him. "Hey! What's with this list? Go here, go there, wait ten minutes. Go aft... go find... tell Joe?"

Without breaking stride, he calmly answered, "Mr. Polevsky has a set pattern he follows, and the Captain wanted you to stay invisible."

I stopped and stared at the paper in my hand. Khan, continued on down the hall with his mission. Wadding up the paper, I threw it at him. "You mean I could have been in my rack this whole time?"

Before turning the corner, he held his watch above his head and pointed to it. "It's time. You're suppose to be on your way to the bridge."

The swells, now so tall, the bow cut into the water as it hit the far side of the trough and anything on deck was being torn at by the sea in an effort to wash it overboard. Staggering through the inside passageways, I waited for the right moment before rushing up the stairs to the bridge, so as not to be thrown back to the bottom.

The Captain motioned me to sit in the empty sonar chair. Staggering past the open charts, I saw the entrance to the Columbia River was circled in red. There was nothing I could do but sit and watch the bar pilot, along with our own pilot, fight with the ship's steering. Sliding into the chair, I lit a cigarette and waited.

An American tug, nothing more than a few lights ahead in the darkness, struggled to pull us over the bar as the river kept trying to spit us out. Sitting in the anchored chair was like a bucking horse ride at a rodeo.

Finally coming abreast of a channel buoy, the bucking quickly subsided. Speculation lead me to believe we were now in the river at that point and that the city of Astoria was our destination.

Relaxing in my chair, thoughts of visiting the coastal area as a youth made me smile. I remembered seeing freighters traveling a few hundred feet from shore before reaching the city where they would anchor a quarter mile or more from shore. Fidgeting in my chair with thoughts of a cold midnight swim ahead of me, I stared out the window of the door. *I need to get off this damn bridge while we're still close to land.*

The south shore was dark, except for an occasional porch light that seemed close enough to illuminate the side of the ship. Grinding my teeth harder and harder as each house light slipped by and the lights of Astoria further up river came into view, I searched for some way out. The bar pilot relaxed at the wheel long enough to empty his cup of coffee. Seeing my chance, I grabbed the pilot's coffee carafe from its rack and shook it. It was empty. "I'll go get you some more."

"Kezel."

"Yes, Captain?" I answered holding onto the door handle wanting to open it and run.

"I need you to come with me. We have more work to do before anchoring." Tossing the grease pencil in his hand on the chart table, he glanced over at the first mate. "Mister Khan, take over while Kezel and I take care of Mister Polevsky's issues."

My eyes got big as I opened the door and he stepped past me. "Put that down and follow me."

A strong breeze blew the rain sideways through the dark night and the cold quickly penetrated my shirt as we walked the outside passageway. "It's cold, sir. I'm goin' to need a coat if we're working outside."

"Follow me. It's all taken care of." At the end of the passage, he stopped at a storage closet. Unlocking it, he held out the bag I had come on board with. "Your coat's in here."

Too cold to figure out what my bag was doing in that closet, I jerked my coat out of it.

Taking off across the open deck toward the back of the ship, the Captain commanded, "There's no time to explain. Bring your gear and let's go."

It was odd that all the lights on the deck were turned off. Normally, the walkway lights would be lit. Working our way in the dark, we seemed to be headed towards the crane used for loading and unloading the ship.

At the crane, he grabbed my arm shoving me against the wall. "We all here?"

I could barely see the two figures in the pitch blackness hunkered down in front of us against the machine. One of them whispered, "Yes."

It was Ivan's voice.

The Captain, letting go of me, grabbed the railing and stared at the blackened shoreline. "The charts say the shore is no more than fifty meters away. We should be able to make—" Suddenly, he pointed to a faint orange glow on shore. "There. We meet at that light." Turning to Ivan, he held a small light over his watch. "In two minutes, this side of the ship should be out of the current and in slack water."

Not having a clue to what was going on, I tied my bag to my waist in hopes that it would act as a flotation device and then grabbed the railing.

Ivan latched onto my bag. "Not yet."

"Now!" The Captain whispered.

Suddenly three more shadowy figures came from around the corner and threw a bundle of net floats over the side. Surprised at seeing more people appear from the darkness, I stepped back watching, as Ivan and the others climbed over the railing and jumped into the water.

"It's our turn." The Captain latched on to my coat and pulled me over the railing as he jumped.

CHAPTER SEVENTEEN

Floating in the dark, the seven of us held onto the crude raft while paddling in the frigid water. Halfway to shore I saw another figure jump off the ship. The lone figure, a stout swimmer, caught up quickly, grabbing onto the raft beside me. Seeing who it was, I tried to welcome him through chattering teeth. "I'mm...mmm...glad you...cou...could join...Missster Khan."

Crawling out of the river, the eight of us made our way over the rocky rip-rap, lining the river bank and gathered around the small oil lantern left on top of a box of blankets. The Captain held out the lantern, "Khan, take this and find the path through that hedge at the top."

I wrapped a blanket around myself and scrambled up the bank after Khan. Finding a path leading into the hedge, Khan set the lantern down on the path and went in. Following him in the darkness, we carefully walked the trail through the thick brush. Stepping into a clearing on the other side, a darkened van sat parked in the beach grass. Khan made a noise like a seagull. The driver jumped out and opened the doors.

The sight of the van made me waffle at going any farther. "I want to thank you guys for including me in your escape... but... I think this is where we go our separate ways."

The Captain, stepping from the hedge, grabbed my arm. "Come on, let's go."

He pulled me to the van's open side doors and shoved me inside. The driver started the engine the moment the Captain climbed in. Stomping on the accelerator as the last door closed, we sped across the sandy opening before he turned on the headlights and followed two ruts through the trees. Exiting the path through the trees, next to a metal warehouse, we turned onto a paved road. Seeing a signpost suddenly lit up by the headlights, I read it out loud, in English. "US

Highway 30." No one said a word. Glancing at the others, I slipped back into speaking Russian. "I always wondered about America."

On the highway, the atmosphere among the seven, seemed to relax. The Captain, taking a pack of cigarettes from a waterproof box in his pocket, held them out as he looked past me. "What happened, Khan?"

After taking one, I looked at Khan. In the light from of an oncoming car I could see his smile. He pulled a kerchief from his pocket and unwrapped the tiger's teeth. "We almost forgot this," he said, handing it to me.

I sat speechless staring at it. Someone who barely knew me, jeopardized their life for a trinket. After tying the talisman around my neck, he patted me on the shoulder. "My mother would never have forgiven me if it was my fault you had lost the Eyes of the Tiger."

We drove over the Young's Bay bridge into the deserted streets of Astoria before I was able to find words. Squinting, as I looked at Khan, I asked, "What do you mean, 'your mother'? You knew the babushka that gave me this?"

Staring out the window at the empty streets, he whispered, "She was everybody's mother."

"That means you know Vasiy, then?"

He didn't answer and continued to stare at the abandoned canneries and fallen down wharves. The highway turned away from the shoreline at a traffic light, and then rambled along one block after another of shuttered or unkept storefronts. Stopping at another red light, I muttered, "Not much different than what we just left, don't you think so, Captain?"

He leaned on his armrest gazing at the sights. "It's still better than prison."

"What's prison got to do with it?"

"The Americans have suspected my ship to be more than a fishing trawler for a long time. Now that they have a chance to inspect her, their suspicions will be confirmed." Taking out a cigarette, he lit it.

"Mister Polevsky and his crew, along with everyone else on board, will be branded as traitors and sent to Moscow."

I blinked at him with disbelief. "What crew? Everyone worked with the fish."

Nicolas piped up from behind. "About a third of those on board worked for Polevsky. Why do you think Mrs. Brevshevnic was brought on. She had the clearances to take their food through the secured hatch and serve them."

"Are you saying," I turned my head trying to see Nicolas behind me, "Moscow sends trawlers into American waters as a cover for spying? And, if they get caught, then, the fishermen have to go to prison too?"

"Son," Ivan spoke up, "didn't you wonder how they found us so fast?" He tapped his brother's shoulder with a flask. "Here, Alex, I think you need some of this."

The Captain took a drink, then handed it to me. Looking at the bottle, I grinned, "No, 'cause America has a superior radar system." Taking a swig, I handed it off to Khan.

"We were just out of their radar range," the Captain snorted. "I gave them our location."

"Ahh, things are beginning to make sense now. The messages, and throwing switches at precise times, it all had to do with our escape. Right, Captain?"

"Don't call me Captain anymore. My name is Alex."

"OK. So...Alex, don't get me wrong, but you guys hardly know me and you didn't need me to pull this off. So, why?"

Alex handed me his pack of cigarettes and a lighter. "I suppose I should inform you of what's really going on."

"You're damn right." I stuffed a cigarette in my mouth. "It's not everyday that eight Russians defect by jumping into the Columbia River."

Mrs. Wrojeck, sitting in the front seat, turned around. "You have it backwards...it was you, who helped the seven of us escape."

"How?" I handed Alex his cigarettes back. "I didn't do any...oh, you mean by killing the engines."

Placing the pack in his pocket, he took a deep breath. "No. In exchange for getting you out of the Soviet Union, we each received fifty thousand American dollars..." he paused, staring at a lone farmhouse as we drove by. "For getting you into the US, we'll each get an additional fifty thousand."

I choked on my cigarette. "What? The American government paid seven hundred thousand for me?"

Krezenski laughed. "Such a short memory. Your government sent you to Siberia, remember?"

"How did you know that? I never said a word to anyone."

"Someone else put up the money." Alex said as he pulled an envelope from his breast pocket and held it up. "While we were at sea, our families in America, got the first payment. When you're delivered to Krezenski's brother, we'll get the other half. And at that time, I am to hand you this envelope."

I held out my hand, palm up.

"Only after you are delivered...not before." He put the envelope back into his pocket and leaned close to me. "It does not indicate in what condition you have to be delivered, so, please don't try anything dramatic."

Not really convinced with their story, I stretched my neck side to side. "OK, what makes you think I am this person of interest?"

Ivan reached forward placing his hand on my shoulder. "Masha was my daughter."

My heart leaped into my throat at the sound of her name. Struggling again with feelings of guilt and sorrow, I stuttered, "I'm...I"m...sorry I...I...couldn't..."

He squeezed my shoulder. "I know. I don't blame you for her death."

Alex smoothed his beard. "She talked about you in her letters to Ivan. She said that you were an American and that had been sent to the work camps by the East Germans. It was her, who came up with the idea that if we could find your family and have them buy your freedom, you would in exchange, help her..." Alex put his fist to his mouth and took a deep breath.

Turning towards him, I glared, "She what?"

He ignored my outburst. "We put out feelers to locate your family through the American consulate, Korean contacts, fishermen in Alaska. Nothing. We didn't realize Romanoff wasn't your given name. Then Krezenski's family, here in the U.S., found that a very connected person had been seeking help through the Russian-American community to locate you. It didn't take long for us to put something together. The only problem was keeping track of you."

Mrs. Wrojeck leaned back in her seat. "When you escaped from the camps, we thought we had lost you."

Half listening to what was said,I wiped my eyes. "Ivan...I'm sorry about Masha. We buried her in a small churchyard overlooking a river. We even had a priest say a prayer for her."

Ivan patted my shoulder. "I know, Katya's letter told me. Thank you, I'm grateful that she was not alone when she died."

"Katya?" I turned looking at Khan.

Khan, turning away from the window, didn't look at me. "It doesn't matter to us why this man wants you back on American soil, only that he is willing to pay."

"How did all of you...I mean I was ready to burn the ship in order to get off. Why didn't you tell me?"

"We couldn't run the risk of Polevsky finding out you were an American. That was the reason for moving you all over the ship." Alex chuckled, "You did a fine job keeping that man totally baffled."

"Almost too good," Pavel thundered. "When you blew up those fuel pumps, you almost got me."

"Wait a minute. I didn't blow up those...ooh...you mean my wiring job."

A flashing red light came from behind the van and began getting brighter and brighter. Slowing down and hugging the shoulder of the road, our driver kept glancing in his mirror. An ambulance flashed past us. Giving a sigh of relief he shook his head and pulled back onto the highway.

We rode in silence until coming to a small town clinging to the hillside above the highway. The young man driving, turned at the first intersection and sped past the town's market, its marquee illuminated a road sign reading, Highway 47. Going up the hill and through town, we passed a school's dimly lit sign. "Hey, Clatskanie! I remember playing that school in sports."

Alex leaned against me. "Those are memories you'll have to put behind you. You know..." he crossed his legs, " according to the American government, you've been dead for several years now. And since you have no American identification to prove who you are, you're a Russian defector... Like us." He handed me the flask in his hand. "Then again, your Russian papers were created out of thin air....Essentially, you do not exist in either country."

"Fucking thanks for reminding me." I emptied remainder of the flask.

Heading through the Oregon back country on the two lane highway, the road was void of any traffic except an occasional log truck headed in the opposite direction. When ever the big rigs passed by, the van rattled and shook. Then one of the trucks pulled wide onto the highway from a side road, making an arc into our lane. Krezenski yelled from the back seat, "Are you sure this is the right road, Peter?"

Gripping the wheel tighter and steering closer to the edge of the pavement, the Peter yelled back, "Trust me, Uncle...we'll be out of the woods in a few minutes."

I turned, looking at Krezenski. "Uncle?"

He chuckled. "The Tzars claimed this part of your country years ago. It won't be long and America's entire Northwest will be ours again."

"Oh, bullshit. I never heard that taught in school."

Nicolas tapped my arm with a thermos. "It's true. Just think, when we get it back...then everyone will have to speak Russian. You'll fit right in, yes?"

Taking the vacuum bottle, I opened it to the smell of coffee instead of vodka. "Well, at least we'll be eating tastier food."

CHAPTER EIGHTEEN

The sun, having risen above the eastern horizon as we pulled in line for the Wheatland Ferry, warmed the inside of the van while we waited for the small car ferry to cross back over to our side of the Willamette River.

A Volkswagen beetle pulled behind us. Then a small school bus filled with children pulled behind the Bug. Peter watched what was taking place behind us in his outside mirror. As the waiting cars began piling up, he looked at his inside rear view mirror. "OK, everyone needs to speak English from now on. We don't need any trouble."

I turned, looking at the Volkswagen. It had a big peace symbol painted on the front and two long-haired hippies sitting inside. "With them?" I laughed. "You gotta be kidding?"

Peter shook his head. "It's been awhile, hasn't it?"

Mrs. Wrojeck tapped Peter's arm, speaking in broken English, "No underrr...umm...stand. OK?"

Peter nodded. Speaking English slowly, he pointed his finger at the first two cars in line."Careful...of...them." Looking back at me in the mirror, he spoke faster, "I'm talking about the mill workers ahead of us. Every time a group of Old Believers get together in public and speak Russian, the police get a call about a Soviet sleeper cell, or that there's spies running around."

"You're joking me?" I chuckled at the thought. "Who would fall for that?"

"A few years ago, a movie named -Telefon-, stirred up a lot of controversy. I call it small town bore—."

The ferry operator tapped on Peter's window. Rolling it down, he handed the operator the money in his hand. "How you doing this morning?"

"Doin' good. Pull to the right of the two in front of ya."

"Sure thing." Peter put the van in gear and drove onto the ferry.

No one spoke the entire time it took to load four more vehicles and cross the river. We more or less gawked at our surrounding like a van load of tourists.

Raising my voice when our front tires touched the pavement on the far riverbank, I asked in English, "Besides Peter and me, who else speaks American?"

My seven co-defectors continued their rubber-necking and didn't answer.

I looked over my shoulder at Ivan. "What about you?"

He shrugged his shoulders.

"Well that's fucking fine," I snarled in English. "You guy's smuggle me into a country and none of you can even speak the fucking language. Shit. Where you taking us Peter?"

Peter, keeping his eyes on the road as he followed the car in front of us through a four-way stop, chuckled, "The store."

Agitated at forcefully being caught up in this circus, I blasted back at him, "For what? To buy clothes?"

He held up his hand, waving it. "Don't worry. Everything's taken care of."

Twenty minutes later we came to a sign saying, 'Welcome to Woodburn'. Sliding forward in my seat looking at the stone and carved wood sign as we passed it, I burst out in English, "Hey, I remember this place. We..."

Alex shifted around in his seat, looking uncomfortable with my outburst.

Sitting back and glancing at him, I switched to Russian. "We used to play sports against the state boy's reform school in this town."

He raised an eyebrow. "You must have traveled quite a bit as a child."

"That would be MacLaren," Peter said as he braked for a red light.

"Yeah, something like that." I picked at the thin mustache growing on my upper lip. "I don't remember its name, but I do remember passing a domed church on the way there."

"That's the one the Old Believers built back in the eighteen hundreds." Peter looked at me in the mirror. "You didn't believe Uncle when he said we've been here for a long time."

"Right under our noses. Why doesn't it surprise me." I took a deep breath and pressed back in my seat. "In fact, after last night, I don't think anything more could surprise me."

Tightening my shoulder muscles and twisting the stiffness out of my neck, I knew that whatever was going to happen at; *The store*, could never compare to the gulags. Yet a nagging in the back of my mind, questioned what to expect from a Russian-American mob boss.

"Here we are," Peter said, as he turned into the parking lot of a tire store. Pulling the van around to the rear of the building, he climbed out and disappeared. The eight of us crawled out and stretched our legs. Peter quickly reappeared to usher us through a door around the corner.

Inside, we entered a room that held a large wooden desk and two brown suede leather couches. A picture of a snowy scene with an onion domed church in the background, hung on one wall of the dark brown wooden paneling. On another wall hung a tire advertisement from the 1950s.

Peter patted one of the couches as he passed by it. "Sit, please." Going over to a table against the wall he put together a pot of coffee. "Coffee 'ill be ready in a minute."

My stomach rumbled at the scent as it brewed. "Oh man," I blurted out, flopping down on the couch. "Nicholas, I actually think I'm going to miss those egg and pork breakfasts of yours."

"Are you saying my cooking is—"

The phone on the desk rang. Everyone froze at the sound. It rang a second time. Peter, filling a bowl with sugar, set the bag down and stared at the phone. It rang a third time, then went silent. Mumbling,

"One...two...three...four..." while counting with his fingers, it rang again as he said, "five."

Picking up the handset, and in almost muted tone, whispered, "Da?" Nodding, he placed the handset on its cradle and looked over at his uncle. "Food will be here in ten minutes. And, father will be here shortly after."

The atmosphere became electrified. The other seven, began speaking as if their part in this business deal was now over.

I looked at Ivan sitting quietly beside me. "What's going on? I thought you guys were staying together?"

"Nope," he said. "I'm going with Alex and Khan to Alaska to be with family up there."

Mrs. Wrojeck excitedly leaned forward reaching over Ivan and tapped my leg. "The three of us...," she pointed to Nicolas, Krezenski, and herself, "are staying here. Pavel is the only one going south with you. His family is in California."

"I ain't going south," I snapped. "I'm going north...to Port—" a knock on the office door stopped my rant.

The door swung open and a young man brought in several bags with a restaurant's logo on them. The familiar scent of eggs and sausages followed him in. The delivery boy opened the bags placing muffins, pastries, apples, oranges, and eight small containers of scrambled eggs and meat patties around the table. Wadding the bags together, he left as quietly as he entered.

The eight of us sat in awe at the perfection of the food before us. Mrs. Wrojeck picked up a piece of fruit. "Look at these apples...there are no worms or bruises."

Nicolas tore open a muffin, "Mmmm...soft and flavorful."

Krezenski grabbed an orange. He sniffed it, then curiously fondled it.

Peter laughed. "What's the matter Uncle, haven't you ever seen an orange before?"

"Never! How do you eat one?"

Before Peter could answer, a grey haired man wearing a white shirt and slacks entered the room. "You have to peel them first..." he stopped in front of Krezenski with his arms wide. "Brother!"

"Joseph!" Krezenski jumped up embracing him.

Two men in polo shirts walked into the room past the brothers and stood at the back of the desk. As they took their place, Joseph stepped away from Krezenski at arms length and looked at his two aides as he pointed, "This is my brother. He is with us finally." With a deep sigh, he patted his brother's shoulders then retreated to his chair behind the desk. "Please, eat while we finish business."

Pulling a metal box from the bottom drawer, Joseph carefully placed it on the desk. Then reaching inside his coat, taking a pack of cigarettes from his shirt pocket, he lit one and leaned back in his chair studying us as we continued to consume the impressive food he provided.

I stared back at him, eyeing the heavy gold chain around his neck. Pulling a muffin apart and stuffing half of it in my mouth, I swallowed it without chewing. Tossing the other half onto the coffee table, I grabbed a soda drink and sucked on the straw. Something I hadn't done in years.

Joseph snapped his finger in front of the associate on his right.

The guy stepped around in front of me, demanding in Russian, "Roll up your sleeves."

Knowing what he was after, I slid my left sleeve up to the elbow.

He grabbed my wrist, pulling my arm closer to his face and inspected the artwork on my arm. "You were in the navy, yes?"

I jerked my arm back and snapped in English, "No! It's the emblem of the Army's Quartermaster Corp. Sheesh, what a fucking dick head."

Joseph's henchman looked rather surprised at my response. Joseph, himself, didn't bat an eye and sat quietly watching me massage my wrist. A few moments later he motioned for his associate to return to his place. Gently folding his hands over his stomach, Joseph spoke in English. "You understand that I have to verify the authenticity of the package, or no one gets paid. Including me."

The late night swim, all night drive, and drinking several cups of coffee along with the sugary pastries, had me edgy, but his insinuation that I was just a bag of spuds for sale, lit my fuse. Jumping up, I snarled, "I don't need you—"

Alex put his hand on my arm. Looking at Joseph, he asked in broken English, "Condition... no concern, yes?"

Joseph nodded his head in confirmation. Dropping back onto the couch, I asked in Russian, "OK. What do you want to know?"

The godfather began playing twenty questions. Some in English, others in Russian. When he was apparently satisfied with all my answers, he opened the metal box on his desk and took out an envelope. "This is your bus ticket." He handed it to one of his henchman. "Your benefactor wants to see you as soon as possible."

The thug came over and shoved it in my face. Snatching the envelope out of his hand, I opened it and took out the Greyhound bus ticket. Joseph pulled a second, thicker envelope from the box, placing it on his desk. "This," he patted the envelope as he looked at me, "is money to buy food along the way." The godfather went back to speaking in Russian. "Alex, I believe it's your turn. You have everything else he needs to know."

Alex handed me the envelope he had in his pocket while Joseph, putting the metal box away asked, "Now who is going with—"

Jumping to the edge of my seat, I shook the blank paper from the envelope that Alex handed me, at the mobster. "What kind of bullshit is this?"

He leaned on his desk gazing at the paper in my hand. "Everything we know about your benefactor...", he scratched his eyebrow with his finger, "is on that paper."

"Bullshit," I yelled. "The only thing on this paper is an address in Phoenix, Arizona."

Alex took the paper from my hand. "He's right. There's not even a name with the address."

"Of course I'm right," I growled. "I can read English. What kind of crap you trying to pull?"

Apparently not used to being challenged by someone he was trying to help, Joseph pushed back in his chair and looked out the window. After a few moments he quietly leaned forward, placing his elbows on his desk and folded his hands. Then with a sigh, he finally looked me in the eyes. "I don't know his name. But, I can say this...do you remember that night in Germany...on the bridge?"

"Like it was yesterday." Crossing my arms across my chest as my back and neck tensed up. "I was traded like a damn sack of potatoes for some asshole senator and an old lady." Fuming with the desire for revenge, I looked at the others. "They," I waved my hand at them, "risked their lives to get me here for the promise of money and their freedom. Give it to them... I'm here. The only thing I want is my life back." Rising to my feet, I grabbed Joseph's cigarettes from the desk. "I'll find the bastard on my own and make him pay." Taking one out, my lips trembled so violently I had trouble keeping it in my mouth. Biting down on the filter, I shoved his pack in my pocket and sat, feeling around my pockets for my lighter.

Joseph quietly watched as I got wound up.

Unable to find my lighter, I glared back at him unconcerned with who he was. Having faced nastier people than him, I wasn't about to back down.

Ivan finally broke the silence. "Might I offer you some advice, son. Forget revenge. Its' bitterness will eat you alive. Look at me..." I turned to see a tear rolling down his cheek. "Masha was my only child...when they came...and took her away, I sought revenge with the help of a bottle." He paused as he sucked in a deep breath through his fingers.

"You were there when she died...and then you then took the life of the man who killed her. How sweet is that memory?"

Joseph motioned to Peter. "Son, get the camera and take pictures of the package for proof of delivery." Handing the henchman on his left a slip of paper, Joseph whispered, "Take them over to Marion's shop and get them their papers."

Watching Peter take several pictures of me, he then scooted his chair back, rose to his feet and tapped the henchman on his right with the back of his hand. "Wire their money as promised." Joseph looked at me with a grandfatherly look, "It would be wise to take your friend's advice and go see who is at that address. Those people down there, are far above yours and mine league."

Stepping around his desk, he shook Alex's hand. "By the time you are done at Marion's, the money will be in your account. It was a pleasure doing business with you, Captain."

* * *

Marion's deli and coffee shop, turned out to be a front for a clandestine printing business where we were given green cards that looked worn and had dates from five years ago.

Looking at the immigration card I was handed, it said my name was Kezel Romanoff, and I was East German. Holding the card up, I flicked it with my finger. "Wow, that sucks."

Joseph's henchman didn't say a word as he handed out social security cards and a small stack of traveler's checks to the others.

"Hey, where's mine?" I asked as he was putting the extras away.

"You don't get one." The thug poked my shoulder with his finger, "Instructions say that you are to only to get enough identification for the ride to Phoenix."

I grumbled sarcastically at him, "Well, that's not very fair."

Watching the others revel in their new found wealth and freedom, I smiled and bit my tongue. *They get to do as they please, but noo...I still have a chain around my neck. Ahh, suck it up, man.*

Shoving my green card in my pocket, I pulled out the pack of cigarettes I had snagged from Joseph. Khan watched me fumble around in an attempt to get one out of the package. He came over and took them from me. "You'll get used to it," he said as he shook one out and handed the pack back. "If you have trouble adjusting, you're welcomed to come to Alaska. Krezenski will know how to find us."

For a man of few words, Khan's offer brightened the moment. "Arrrgh, matey. Yous right." I bit down on my cigarette and patted him on the back. "Hows 'bout we have one last meal together 'fore the bus arrives?"

Khan rolled his eyes, "And to think, Brother chose you to be the next in line."

Alex, putting his papers in his pocket, smiled for the first time. "What a grand idea. Marion, do you have a place for us?"

Marion nodded and ushered us into a private room next to the kitchen. His wife served us like royalty the whole time, never letting our cups run dry, nor our plates sit empty. Finally, after about an hour, she leaned close to Pavel as she filled his cup. "I am to remind you, the Greyhound bus will arrive in ten minutes. It stops in front of the deli only long enough to pick up and drop off."

Pavel nodded, then stood. "Time to go, Kezel. I can't wait to see my son."

Quickly shaking everyone's hand, I followed Pavel out the door.

Standing on the sidewalk and leaning against the bus sign, I glanced at my watch. "Oh yeah. If you don't mind, I want to make a side trip to Fresno to give a friend's mother, his belongings. This letter and wallet."

Pavel smiled. "Sure, after we get to LA."

"She lives north of LA. It would be easier to do it first, ."

"Deal." He offered me his hand. His grip was excruciating. Wincing at the pain, I tried to pull free. Stronger, Pavel pulled me close. "After we get to LA. Yes?"

"OK. OK."

He let go and patted me on the back. "I knew you'd see it my way."

For the entire twenty two hours it took Greyhound to get us to LA, Pavel never let me out of his reach. And as much as it should have annoyed me, I actually felt amused as I translated what was in English, into Russian for him.

Arriving in the LA terminal, Pavel led the way off the bus whispering his son's name in a rhyming tune. Figuring this was the last I'd see of him, I started singing along with him as we walked towards the door. He stepped off first and as soon as my foot touched the ground, he had me by the arm, pulling me down the line of buses like a piece of luggage.

I tried jerking away. "Let go of me, I can walk."

"Nothing personal, but for a hundred thousand...I'm not taking any chances."

Digging in my heels and forcing him to stop. "OK, OK, I get the point. I promise you. I won't run."

He loosened his grip, but didn't entirely let go. "I hope you understand..." Rising up on his toes, he looked down the row of buses, "It's just that the money's already been paid."

I patted my shirt pocket. "You wouldn't happen to have a smoke? I'm out."

He pulled a pack of Russian cigarettes from his jacket. "Here, I was saving these for my son, but not anymore."

"Heh, heh, no you keep 'em. There's a vending machine over there—"

"No, I insist. Here." He shoved them into my hand. "Besides, that is your bus right over there, yes?"

I glanced over to where he was looking, "Yeah, right. If you say so."

With my sleeve still in his grip, he guided me through the crowd towards a bus that said -*Chartered*- on its marquee. Holding out his hand to the driver, Pavel asked, "How are you, brother?"

Astonished at his sudden use of English, but even more so at the choice of his words, I watched their handshake. Recognizing it from the gulags as the Brotherhood's means of identification, I grinned, shoving out my hand. "How are you, brother?"

Pavel intercepted, slipping me a folded envelope. "Give him."

Holding my hand out to the driver, he gripped it and looked at my escort. "He is in good hands now. May you have a pleasant journey."

Pavel grinned, "A moment." Taking a small camera out of his pocket, he clicked three pictures of me and the bus driver as we smiled and shook hands. Then several more as the driver put his arm around my shoulder and shoved me up the steps.

I heard Pavel holler, "Thank you," before disappearing.

At the top of the steps the driver slipped the envelope into his shirt pocket, then pointed, "We have a special seat for you. Right, behind mine. Once we're on the way, I am authorized to answer any of your questions."

The velour seat felt inviting as I looked around the virtually empty bus. I squirmed backward into the plush seat, asking in Russian, "Not many people travel by bus anymore, yes?"

Looking at me in his mirror as the engine rumbled to life, he answered in English, "This one's chartered. Just for you."

CHAPTER NINETEEN

Leaning back in my seat, I watched the LA scenery slowly turn from houses stacked upon each other, to bare desert covered with sage and tumbleweed. Out of habit I pulled a cigarette from the pack Pavel had given me and lit it. The driver looked at me in his mirror. "You're not allowed to smoke on buses anymore, even chartered ones. Put it out."

"Hey, this is a special imported brand." I held the pack up for him to see. "Stop and let me off so I can finish it."

The driver watched me in his mirror wave the pack around.

"If that's mary jane, you need to put it ou—"

Suddenly he jerked the bus into the fast lane narrowly missing a Volkswagen van covered with stickers and painted flowers creeping along the Interstate. He hit the horn as we passed and snarled, "Damn freaks. Their garbage cause more accidents."

I took another puff. "You got an ash tray, or you gunna stop and let me off?"

He patted the envelope in his breast pocket. "We're non-stop. Put it out, or go use the toilet in the back like everyone else."

Walking towards the back of the bus, I counted six other people on board; Four men and two women. They all turned their heads away, ignoring me as I walked by. Reaching for the doorknob, I muttered audibly, "Sheesh, it's already started. Like I ain't even here."

Stepping in and locking the door behind me, I couldn't help but marvel at how many conveniences were crammed in such a small place. After trying them all out, I opened the door, "Oh yeah...life's gunna be diff—, Someone has changed seats."

I glanced at the six other passengers as I stood in the back. Twisting the corner of my mustache, I smiled, "OK, got it." I pointed at her, "The grey haired woman in the black tweed outfit. She was sitting by herself, working out of a briefcase. And now she's moved next to the only other person not wearing a Greyhound uniform." Softly, I mimicked a movie idle, "Ahhh, number one son, you 'ave done well. Someday you have show of your own." I headed for my seat.

As I approached the row the grey haired woman sat in, I heard her whisper a single word to the man beside her. Looking up and seeing me, he quickly shoved his hand inside his suit coat. I caught the glint of a metallic reflection as he was moving. Stopping, I casually stared him in the eyes. He pulled his hand out and folded his arms across his chest looking away. Yawning in a mocking fashion, I slowly proceeded towards my seat studying each of the other four occupants.

At my seat, I raised the dividing armrests and flopped sideways onto the seat. "I thought you said this bus was just for me?"

"It is. They're relief drivers. They'll be getting off soon."

"What about the two not wearing company uniforms?"

"Don't know. They came with the bus."

"Uhm...K." I leaned towards the driver. "So who's paying for this ride?"

"It's on the paper you were handed earlier."

"Ssst. All it had was an address. And addresses mean nothin', names do." Sitting back in my seat, I pulled the paper from my shirt pocket. "However, since there ain't no name on it, who's paying for all this?"

Reaching over, he took his coffee cup from its holder. "Can't answer that one." Holding the cup above his shoulder, he shook it. "You mind pouring me some from that thermos?" I reached for the steel container as he continued. "I do know...that the address belongs to a law firm. That's where I'm supposed to drop you off at."

"You joking me?" I twisted off its cap and poured his coffee. "Some outfit hunted me down over a parking ticket that I skipped out on years ago?"

The driver chuckled, glancing up in the mirror. "If only that were the case."

"Then what is the case?" I handed him his cup. "You said you'd answer my questions."

"So I did." He took a sip. "I was told to give that address as an answer to any question you asked. There's another cup in the rack, you're welcomed to have some and relax."

I leaned back, closing my eyes. "No thanks."

The hiss of air-brakes, along with jerking of the bus, woke me from my slumber as it came to a complete stop, Sitting up, I looked around. We had stopped at a truck stop in the middle of nowhere. Three of the four uniformed employees were lined up to get off.

I leaped to my feet to follow them.

A hand from behind, gripped my collar. "Sit down."

Twisting and jabbing my elbow backwards in an effort to strike my assailant, it turned out his arms were longer than mine. He threw me back into my seat, hitting my head on the window. A burly guy in a company uniform dropped into the seat next to me and folded his arms across his chest.

Sitting up, I rubbed my head. "Sheesh, What's your problem?"

The driver climbed out of his seat and looked at me. "You need to do what Carl tells you." He straightened his collar and partially zipped his jacket. "Anything I can get you from the cafe?"

Pushing myself away from the window, I snarled, "Yeah, a name."

"Sorry can't help you there." He grabbed his thermos. "A soda? Burger?"

"Fine," I growled.

The driver looked inside the thermos then poured what was left into his cup. "Which?"

"Both."

"Cheese?"

"Sure."

"Fries or chips?"

"Fries."

"Ketchup?"

I looked out the window. "You ask too many fucking questions."

"What makes you think that? I'm just trying to get you what you want."

Whipping around and glaring at him, I growled, "You know...where I just spent the last four fucking years, the only choice I had was; Eat the shit they threw on your plate or starve."

He held up his hands. "Hey, don't shoot the messenger." Grabbing the small bag of trash next to his seat, he stood at the top of the stairs. "I'm just getting paid to deliver. You want something to eat or not?"

Scrunching my shoulders and stretching my back muscles, I muttered, "Sorry. You need money?"

"My treat. Your usual, Carl?"

Carl nodded as the driver walked down the steps.

"If we're gunna be here a while..." I pulled out a cigarette and lit it.

Carl growled clearing his throat.

"What?" Waving my hand around in circles in front of myself, I looked at him. "You told me to sit. I can't get off, so where the hell can I smoke?"

He made the guttural sound again.

"OK, OK, I get it." Pulling out the pack, I shook one up for him. "Careful, they're Russian."

As he reached for it, I jerked the pack away. "I don't know...they might be too strong for you."

Snatching the pack from my hand, he put one in his mouth. I held out my lighter and took the pack from his hand. Carl inhaled deeply, tilted his head back and started blowing smoke rings. He had an uncanny ability to create perfect rings each time. Watching him was more entertaining than looking out the window.

When I finished with mine, I dropped it on the floor and stepped on it. "You know Carl, I knew a guard in East Germany that I think you would like. The two of you could sit in silence and carry on an entire conversation."

He flicked his cigarette out the open door.

"No...I mean it. I—"

The toilet door in the back, slammed shut distracting me. Glancing over the back of the seats, I noticed the business woman's companion was still in his seat, but she wasn't.

"I got you a ham sandwich and chips," the driver said as he climbed up the steps. "It would have taken them an hour to cook you a burger with that crowd."

I turned back around as the driver handed Carl a bag.

Carl opened the bag, looking in. "Where's the drinks?"

The driver produced two cans of soda from his coat pockets and tossed them to me. Sliding into his seat, he fired up the engine. "We're behind schedule."

"What about the others..." I popped open a can, "you gunna wait for them?"

"They're relief drivers for other buses." He looked in his mirror. "Where's the woman?"

"She's in the toilet," Carl mumbled, handing me the bag.

Pawing through the bag, I glanced at Carl, "She work for the company, too?"

"Naw, don't know who she is." He looked at the driver. "All we know...is her and her friend are supposed to get off at the same address as you."

"Great, I'll go back and talk to them after I'm done eating."

Carl swallowed the soda in his mouth. "Nope, can't do that. Not suppose to talk to anyone but Lonnie here."

I put a chip in my mouth and cringed at its saltiness. "This whole talking thing is starting to get fucking annoying."

Lonnie turned down the ramp onto the Interstate. "Two more hours and you'll get your answers. Eat your sandwich and relax."

Finished with my sandwich and chips, I looked back to see if the woman had come out yet. *Nope. Still in the shitter.* Staring at her companion, I noticed he hadn't moved since we stopped. "Hey, Lonnie. You mind if I smoke here? Apparently she's still in the toilet."

He looked up in his mirror. "Carl, go check on her. See if she needs something."

I crushed my can. "Yeah, tell her I need to take a piss, too."

Carl got up, dropped his food wrappers in the trashcan next to Lonnie, then walked back. "Hey, mister. You OK?"

I turned in my seat watching as Carl tapped the guy. "Hey, Lonnie, this guy's dead. There's a knife in his chest."

I jumped up, stepping into the aisle. "Where's the woman?"

Carl shrugged. "Her briefcase is still here next to the guy."

"Lonnie, turn this damn bus around and call the police," I yelled. "She had to have done it."

The toilet door flew open. Stepping out, the woman raised her hands and shot Carl, twice. He crashed into a heap in the aisle.

Lonnie yelled at me, "Get on the steps."

I grabbed the handrail support pole and swung feet first down the stairs as she fired a third round. It ricocheted off the pole just above my hands.

"Why did you have to come back?" she screamed. Pulling the trigger again, this time she hit the windshield above my head. "You were suppose to die."

"What the fuck are you talking about?" I yelled from the stairwell.

"You weren't supposed to come back, you were supposed to die in their damn prison."

I peeked down the aisle around the base of the pole. "How the hell do you know who I am?"

Propped against a seat steadying herself, she pointed the pistol at me. A bullet ripped into the floor at the top of the steps. Ducking back down in the stairwell, I looked over at Lonnie. Something about him didn't seem right. He was half hunched over the wheel. "Hey, Lonnie, you OK?"

It looked like he was shaking his head, but I couldn't tell with the swaying of the bus. Keeping an eye on Lonnie, I yelled, "Who the hell are you?"

"That night on the bridge...you had to go and grab Senator Bernard's arm and whine. You should have sucked it up and done your duty like you were suppose to."

"I remember that guy...and some old woman, but I don't remember you." I slid up the wall to peek over the railing. "Wait a minute...you said he was a senator?"

Another round went through the windshield above my head.

"I worked my whole life for that ungrateful bastard. I loved him and slaved for him my entire life. Then, he said was going to give that worthless asshole Allen, a position on the board instead of me." She put a round through the door above my head.

"Who the hell is Allen?" I looked over towards Lonnie for something to throw at her. "And why are we going to that address?"

Another bullet went through the front row seats, denting the steel plate I was hiding behind.

"You're not going anywhere. You're going to die like you were supposed to."

Cringing down lower on the steps, I pressed my back on the door. "At least tell me who wants to kill me?"

"The Army declared you dead. I was there when they buried you. Then I tried to get him to forget about you." Another round ricocheted off the handrail, taking out the door window. "But noooo. You had to come back."

"Hey lady, we're on the same side. I want to get even with that senator, too." Bending over, I lit a cigarette. "Whatta you say we work together."

"I'm listening. Stand up and talk to me."

"OK." I raised the cigarette above the steel plating.

She tried to hit it, putting her last round through the windshield.

"That was eight, you're out." Climbing up the steps, I reached over to help Lonnie.

"You think I'm stupid because I'm a woman? Guess again." She ejected the empty clip and slipped in another one. The next bullet struck Lonnie in the back.

I let go of his lifeless body. It dropped onto the steering wheel, jerking the bus towards the shoulder of the freeway. The vehicle struck a guardrail, ripping the door off as it destroyed the steel railing.

The impact knocked me down the stairs. Unable to grab onto anything, I tumbled out the open door, hitting the sandy soil hard bouncing out of the path of the rear wheels and coming to rest against a sage bush. The bus raced full throttle out into the desert.

Laying in the sand, I heard the screech of twisting, tearing metal, suddenly the engine raced for what seemed like eternity, followed by a muffled roar of igniting fuel.

In the quiet darkness, I lay there rubbing my chest where the tiger's teeth around my neck had scratched me. "Ahh Babushka, where were your tigers?"

Finally getting up, I could see light from the burning bus dancing in the distance. Wiping my face with my sleeve, I swallowed real hard as I looked around in the moonlight. Seeing nothing that might help me, I followed the trail of destroyed vegetation back to the freeway.

Stepping onto the pavement, I lit a cigarette and looked eastward towards Phoenix. Turning and looking to the west, there off in the distance, were a set of headlights coming my direction.

Walking towards the lights, I lit my lighter and waved my arms. The headlights stopped next to me and the side door slid open. I looked at the painted flowers and stickers all over the V-dub van. Shrugging with indifference to Lonnie's words, I climbed in.

CHAPTER TWENTY

The two hippies didn't say a word as I climbed in the back of their van. The guy driving, stared straight ahead tapping his fingers on the steering wheel, while the girl riding shotgun nodded her head with the rhythm of the music blaring from the eight-track stereo. I nestled down into the pile of beanbag chairs they used for back seats and kept an eye on them while enjoying the sudden lack of attention.

Sometime after midnight, we pulled in front of a house on the south side of Phoenix. The twenty-something girl got out and went straight into the house. The driver came around and slid the side door closed after I climbed out. "You're welcome to come inside and crash with the rest of us, dude."

"Thanks," I muttered, following him towards the house.

In the front room were half a dozen bodies already asleep on the two couches and the floor. My host, stepping over a few of them as he walked towards a hallway, pointed, "Bathroom's on the left. Don't worry about privacy, we're all adults."

I snickered thinking of the open urine barrel in the gulags. Glancing around in the dim light, I spied an unoccupied corner on the other side of the room. Making my way around the sleeping bodies, I laid down in the empty space trying to get as comfortable as the concrete floor under the carpet would allow.

Vivid dreams of what happened on the bus tormented my slumber, until gasping for breath, I sat up. *Where the fuck am...Oh, that's right. Who the hell was she?* Wiping at the sweat on my face, I laid back down. *Well, at least I won't have to worry about her anymore. I doubt she made it off the bus.*

Asleep once more, dreams of the woman crawling out of the burning wreckage and waving her flaming fist in my face, had me thrashing about in my sleep trying to keep her away. The putrid smoke from her burnt flesh, suddenly, had a calming effect. Relaxing as I inhaled the pungent aroma, the woman faded away, allowing me to slip into a blissful slumber.

I woke up the next morning, to an odd smell mixed with the scent of coffee. All I could see was black hair covering my face. Pushing myself up into a sitting position and rubbing my eyes, the black lab, who's tail was laying across my face, crawled onto my lap and licked me.

"Don't." I pushed him away wiping at the slobber clinging to my face. "Whoa, what a night."

A voice from around the corner, offered, "Would you like a cup of coffee?"

I flopped over onto my side, poking my head past the edge of the wall and looked into the kitchen area. Two young women in over-sized T-shirts sat at the table. The girl from the van stood next to the coffee pot with an empty cup in her hand.

"Please," I groaned. "How do I get this dog off me?"

One of the girls at the table giggled. "His name's Lassie." She got up and opened the sliding glass door to the backyard. "Come on Lassie, let's go."

The one from the van placed the cup on the table before an empty chair. With Lassie off of me, I crawled to the chair and climbed in. "Ohhh, that smells good."

Grabbing a plate of toast from the counter, she sat down across the table from me. "Somebody kicked you out in the middle of the desert, huh?"

I held the cup up to my nose masking my mouth. "You might say that."

Spreading some butter on a slice of toast, she glanced at me. "That is...where we found you."

The rancid smell of hot butter made me cringe. "Uhm, the bus made an unscheduled stop and I got off."

Putting her elbows on the table, she cradled her chin in her palm and stared at me. "Oh really?"

"OK." I twisted around in my chair trying to get comfortable. "Actually I was invited to speak with a Senator Bernard about investing in solar energy." Leaning on the table, I gave her a sarcastic smile. "And, I didn't realize the two guys giving me a ride from Blythe, worked for a petrol company. When I told them why I was headed to Phoenix, they dumped me in the middle of bum-fuck-Egypt, claiming they were on their way to work. They took off so fast, I didn't even have a chance to get my backpack outta their truck"

Sitting back, she broke a second slice in two. "Not bad. Did it hurt?"

"Yes, it was a long walk...ahh...what are you talking about, did it hurt?"

"I know the road." She took a bite of her toast. "But I doubt that you're here to see the Senator."

"What makes you think that?" I pulled the paper with the address on it from my pocket and held it up. "This is my invite to speak with him."

She laughed as she dipped her toast in her coffee. "How long ago was that?"

Cramming the paper into my pocket, I picked up my cup. "Just recently."

One of the other girls looked at their friend. "I don't think he knows, Penny."

Penny sat back putting her heel on the seat of her chair and placed her chin on her knee. "He's been in a private hospital over in Scottsdale for the last three months."

"We gotta be talking about two different people." I drained the rest of my coffee and set the cup down. "I got the invite, like...two weeks ago."

"Nope, my cousin works there. I've met him several times when I've gone over to see her." A tear rolled down Penny's cheek. "Cancer is tearing him apart and he doesn't have long."

I shoved my chair away from the table. "If that's the case, I better go now."

Penny, wiping her nose with her hand, shook her head. "No, no, have some breakfast first."

Able to glean the whereabouts of the hospital, along with the Phoenix bus routes in general as Penny dished up a plate of toast and eggs for me. I was about to ask a pointed question about Bernard, when she slid the plate across the table and asked, "What's your name? We don't even know your name."

"Uhh...It's Bud."

Penny snorted as she looked at the girl who had let Lassie out, "What did I say, Sally? Ok, Uhh Bud. Where you from?"

Stuffing egg in my mouth to avoid answering, I pointed to my cup.

"Wow, you nailed it, Pen." Sally shook her head as she poured more coffee in my cup. "What are you running from...Uhh Bud?"

I swallowed, then washed the eggs down with the coffee. Pulling out my cigarettes, I placed one between my lips and tossed the pack on the table. Reaching for my lighter, Penny leaned across the table. "Please don't light that in here."

Taking it from my lips, I sighed loudly and stuck the cigarette behind my ear.

"We have to smoke 'em outside in the backyard," Sally crowed.

The third girl picked up the package of cigarettes and studied the Cyrillic writing on it. "What kind of brand are these?"

"I knew it." Sally snatched them from her. "Your secret's safe with us, Bud...da."

Holding out my hand, I snapped my fingers. "I bought 'em in a tobacco shop in LA."

Penny flipped her hair over her shoulder, tilted her head eyeing me. "Is that really your name?"

"Sure." I rose to my feet, taking the cigarette from behind my ear and held it out. "Now if you don't mind."

Playing with Lassie in the backyard gave me time to lay out a plan while the women were in the kitchen finishing breakfast. One at a time they disappeared from the kitchen. With no one to see me, I slipped out the back gate and down the alley.

Walking out to the street, I could see a bus stop several blocks away on the corner. A city bus pulled up just as I got there. Climbing the stairs, I held out a five dollar bill, "You goin' towards Scottsdale?"

The driver pointed across the street, "He'll be here in about five minutes."

Crossing the street, a woman waiting at the stop, covered her nose as I sat down on the bench. Sneering, I grabbed my pant leg and shook it. "Slipped and fell in a pile of dog crap."

As the bus worked its way towards Scottsdale, we stopped next to a Union Gospel Mission. As the bus pulled away, I caught a whiff of myself. I did smell like crap. Jumping up, I jerked on the notification cord several times, "Hey! Wait! Stop!"

He pulled over and opened the doors. As I rushed past him, the driver muttered, "You only have to pull it once," then shut the doors, clipping me on the the backside.

At the mission hall I got a hair cut, showered, picked up some clean clothes, then stood in line for a meal. One of the volunteers dishing out the meal saw the Eyes of the Tiger around my neck and started heckling me. "What res did you just come from? Or you been robbin' graves up in the hills?"

Baring my teeth, I drew a finger across my throat and hissed, "Ayes rips 'em froms da tiger's mouth wid me's bair hands."

"Careful, Popeye. They have a place for your kind over in Mesa." Turning and grabbing another stack of plates, he muttered, "Damn fruit cake."

After eating, I caught the next bus headed towards the Paradise Valley area of Scottsdale where Penny said the private hospital was. Feeling edgy about not knowing when to get off, I thought of asking the driver. Then I noticed the route map painted on the curvature between wall and ceiling. I banged the seat with my knuckles, *Ooh, damn lucky. Off at the next stop...east towards 51, then north to Scott's drive...*

The stop was by a gas-station with a food market. Having twenty minutes before the connecting bus, I went inside. Walking around looking for a bottle of vodka, I saw a display of ice picks next to a cardboard cut-out of a polar bear near the checkout.

I snatched one and slid the wooden sheath off the pencil-thin steel rod. Touching its needle sharp point, I put it back together and threw it on the counter. "A pint of vodka, too," I muttered.

"What kind?"

"I don't care."

The clerk rang up the pick. "You have to tell me which one. I can't choose for you."

"Just grab one."

"I don't know...you old enough?"

Running my fingers through my freshly cut hair, I snapped, "Give me the one with the red label that says Moose-cows."

"Moskva...that'll be five twenty five."

Tossing a ten on the counter, I shoved the pick and liquor bottle in my pocket. Seeing the bus pull up, I ran out the door.

"Hey, your change!"

"Keep it," I yelled, running for the bus.

It was mid-afternoon by the time the bus came to its stop just down the street from the hospital. Stepping out from the cool air in the bus to the eighty-five degree afternoon heat made it plain I didn't need to wear a jacket. For some reason, figuring the jacket made me look like a local, I left it on.

Standing in the shade of a tree, I smoked a cigarette and surveyed the two story building. On the far side of the parking lot sat a bench on a little patch of grass under a citrus tree. *That's gotta be the best spot until*

I figure out what and who. If I'm lucky the oranges 'ill be ripe and can tide me 'til dinner.

Crossing the parking lot, I plucked a low hanging fruit from another tree. Admiring the texture of the large yellow fruit, I bit into the rind to peel it. "Ahg, phuff...Damn, a lemon! Didn't know they got that big." Dropping the lemon on the bench, I pulled what I hoped to be an orange from the tree growing next to it and sat down. Looking at the front doors, I whispered, "Perfect. From here I can see everything through those glass doors."

Fruit in hand, I studied the orange while keeping an eye on the front desk. The woman at the desk missed nothing, making everyone sign in or out. Biting a hole in the orange's rind, I began sucking the juice out. "She's gotta go pee, eat lunch...do somethin', she can't sit there forever."

Someone crossing the parking lot caught my attention. It was a nurse walking through the parking lot towards her car, "Where the fuck did she come from. She didn't go through the front door."

Flinging the orange to the ground, I wiped my hands on my pants. A second nurse hurried from the side of the hospital, making a hasty scramble for her car. After both cars left, I ambled across the lot and around the corner of the building, spotting an exit door fighting against the inside air pressure to close.

Carefully listening for footsteps in the stairwell, I slipped in and quickly pulled the door closed. Tip-toeing to the fire-door leading into the hallway, through its tiny window, a linen cart was visible. Two clipboards hung from its side. With no one in sight, I peeled off my jacket and used it to keep my fingerprints off the door.

Sticking my head in the hall and hearing undecipherable chatter coming from different rooms, I stepped into the corridor and flipped my jacket over my shoulder, casually sauntering towards the cart. Skimming through the names on both clipboards, neither a Bernard, or a Richards, was listed. "Damn," I hung them back in place. Spinning around to go hide in the stairway, I slammed into a nurse carrying an arm load of laundry.

"I'm sorry. I'm so sorry," Reaching down, I offered to help the girl up. Looking at her candy striped uniform, I blurted out, "It's my fault, I wasn't paying attention."

Waving my hand away, she rolled onto her knees and gathered the folded sheets scattered about. "It's good thing I wasn't carrying a bed pan."

My face flushed with the thought. Stammering, "I'm...I'm..." I picked up the three farthest sheets, placing them on her stack. "I'm looking for my boss's client. I was supposed to pick up some papers from him and deliver them a half-hour ago."

"No harm." She stood up squeezing the sheets tight to her chest. "So..." she looked me up and down, "who you looking for?"

Staring into her eyes, I smiled, "A Mister Bernard Richards. Or, it might be Richard Bernard."

"Mister Bernard is upstairs in room 238. He's such a nice gentleman. It's so unfortunate..." she dumped the sheets in her arms onto the cart, "that he's in such bad shape. You know he's—"

Smiling, I put my hand on her arm. "I know, isn't it? But, I have to get those papers before...you know, the boss kills me." I stepped around her. "Oh, where's the stairs?"

"At the end of the hall, through the exit door."

"I just came from there, I didn't see any." Shifting my jacket to my other arm, the ice pick fell out of its pocket to the floor. Scrambling to retrieve it, I shoved the steel rod into its sheath and covered it with my jacket. "Would you mind showing me?"

The cute aide pulled the cart between us. "I can't. I have to get Miss Arthur's bed made so she can take her medication." Grabbing a sheet, she ducked into the next room.

Briskly walking to the end of the hall and up the stairs to the next floor, I stood looking through the door's window for a moment. The fire door squeaked, killing the silence as I cracked it open. Poking my head into the empty hallway, I shoved the door open and scurried down the corridor checking room numbers as I went.

A pill cart sat outside room 237. I could hear its occupant arguing with the nurse about having to take so many pills. Scanning the clipboard on the cart, Bernard was next on the list. Not wanting to be seen in his room, I retreated back to the stairwell.

Sitting on the top step waiting, I took a couple swigs of vodka to calm my nerves. My throat caught on fire. Wiping at my mouth with my sleeve and swallowing hard to get the fire to recede, I crammed the bottle into my pocket.

Crawling over and peeking into the hallway. The cart was gone. Scrambling to Bernard's door, I put my ear to it.

Silence.

Slipping into the dimly lit room, I stared at the person in the bed. Stepping closer, I checked the name on the chart hanging at the foot of the bed.

There, in bold letters was; **Richard Bernard**.

The figure lying before me looked frail and thin, yet his face was still what I remembered. The one who snatched my life, causing the nightmare I couldn't escape from.

Looking at him through the tangle of hoses and wires attached to his body keeping him alive, I tried to decide what to do. His breath was shallow. The heart monitor beeped a constant rhythm. Not sure that just pinching a hose would make him feel the pain I wanted him to, I glanced around the room for another option. On the far side of the room was a tray with several vials and a syringe. Walking past the beeping machines to the tray, I looked at the label of both vials, they were full of morphine. Remembering the sensation of using the drug from days past in Germany, I held them whispering, "For me...or for him? For me...or for him?" I picked up the syringe. "The simplest thing would be to give him both." Using both vials to filled it, I reached for the port in his IV line. "Since I'm dead and don't exist, there's no way they can trace it back to me." Shoving the needle in, I mouthed, "And...no one will ever know."

A hand zipped out from under the sheet gripping my wrist.

"Wha...the fuck?" I tried jerking my arm free, but his grip was like that of a steel trap.

Opening his eyes slowly, he whispered in a hoarse voice, "You made it."

"You're damn right I did." I managed to twist my arm free. "And you're gunna regret it."

"Why? You going to kill me?" He coughed. "You push that plunger and I won't feel a thing. I'll die with a smile."

I bit my lip, wanting him to feel my pain. To squirm. To feel the fear I felt. "Mother fucker, you're gunna feel this." I reached for the ice pick in my back pocket. It wasn't there. I glanced around the floor while keeping an eye on him.

He coughed again, then wheezed, "The nightmare, I've been paying for all these years. I'm sorry you got caught up in my selfish greed."

Violently shaking my fist at him, I screamed, "Your nightmare! It was I who went to prison. I was the one who watched his best friend get ripped to shreds by a tank."

He grabbed hold of my wrist again.

Trembling, I fought, trying to speak. "And...and...watched...his girl friend... slaughtered...by an asshole...for..."

Bernard squeezed my hand. "I'm sorry, I didn't mean for it to happen. Can you forgive me?"

"Forgive you?" Snarling, I stepped away from the bed. "Four years of my life, gone. My future snatched from me. Why? Ha ha, so a mother fuckin' politician could make his wife happy. Forgive you, fuck you." Snatching my jacket from the floor, I searched through it for the ice pick. "Do you know how many Americans died in those camps because of you fucking assholes in DC?"

Bernard pushed on the bed controls, raising himself into an upright position. "Yes, I do know. My father was one of those abandoned after World War Two. When I saw your tattoo, I realized you were one of us and not some Russian kid needing to be repatriated." Coughing, he wiped his mouth. "I wore on my collar the same insignia you have on your arm. As an officer, I took the same oath you did. No one left behind." Gasping and wheezing, he struggled to breath, "I...couldn't...leave you there."

I threw my jacket at the door. "You did a fine fucking job at doing just that."

"How do..." with one hand he held the oxygen tube under his nose as he turned his head towards me, "you think you got back here?"

Pulling the scrape of paper with the address on it from my pocket, I shook the crumpled wad at him. "Some lawyer bought my freedom."

Bernard gurgled in his attempt at laughing. "My lawyer. I used...my position...in Congress to find you. I was...labeled a communist sympathizer...and lost my seat in the Senate."

"So fucking what." I fumbled with a cigarette. "I lost my name, my family, my life."

"I wouldn't light that...it will bring the nurses." He struggled for more breath. "I was so focused...on finding you...I neglected my own wife. Then after...you were located, I spent...most of my wealth...to get...you back." A tear rolled down his cheek as he struggled to breath, "She left me last year. I almost...missed...her fune...funeral."

I stood there staring at the shell of a man who once had everything, wealth, power, notoriety, and gave it up in an effort to right a wrong he had done. Sucking in a deep breath between my teeth, I felt the humbleness in his words and offered, "I'm sorry about your wife."

Things got quiet as I put the cigarette away in my pocket. Still confused, my emotions continued fighting over seeking the bitter taste of revenge, or agreeing with Nicolas that maybe the man before me, had suffered as much as I.

Bernard pointed a finger at the cabinet on the other side of his bed. "There's an envelope for you in that drawer. Would you mind?"

Nodding, I walked over and opened the drawer. A brown envelope with the NorthStar Corporate logo embossed on it along with the handwritten name Kezel Romanoff, lay in the drawer. Picking up the envelope, I could feel papers and a key inside.

"My wife and I had no children. I feel...after the last few years...I know you well...and would...'ave...been proud—"

"Bullshit. You don't know me." I dropped the envelope back in the drawer. "You never met me before that day."

"I talked...your sergeants...both gave me faith...you have...strength to survive. An...you did. I'm grateful—" He choked while gasping for more air. "Please...the letter."

I picked the envelope back up and shook it at him. "Are you trying to buy my forgiveness?"

"No...I'm asking for it." The empty syringe fell to the floor from his hand. "Please."

I bit my lip at seeing it.

"Take it...to...address...on paper. They...know wha...to..." Bernard coughed as the monotonous beep of the heart monitor began slowing down. "I'm sorry."

Dropping the letter, I grabbed the IV line, pinching it an effort to stop the flow. "No! You can't die yet."

His eyes began to flutter. "Go...go."

Taking hold of his hand, I looked him in the eye, "Damn it, don't die. I forgive you."

His eyes closed as he mouthed, "Thank you."

The beeping from the monitor slowed even more.

"Fuck." Laying his hand gently on his chest, I scooped up the letter and rushed to the door. Picking up my jacket, I put it on, then stuffed the envelope inside my sleeve around my arm. Glancing once more at him before opening the door, his breath made a soft squeaking sound. I stepped into the hallway and raced for the stairs. The monitor's flat-line alarm above his door squealed to the world of his passing before I got to the bottom of the stairwell.

Bursting out the exit door, I ran around the corner, across the parking lot and down the street to the bus stop. Where I melted into a pile on the bench, withdrawing from the world. The late afternoon air cooling as the sun touched the tops of the mountains, I sat mulling over what had just happened. Buses came and went. The street lights flickering as they turned on, a bus pulled up and opened its door. "Hey buddy! I'm the last one if you want a ride."

Looking around at my options, I climbed the steps while fumbling in my pocket for the fare. A group of young people standing around a building across the street laughing, caught my attention. "What's going on over there?" I asked.

"What?" The driver handed me my ticket and change as he glanced across the street. "Uhh, that's an evening church service."

I spun around. "Open the door."

"But—"

"Keep it. I want off."

The bus stayed at the curb as I raced across the street in front of it.

Walking into the church I sat in the back row, still not sure why I got off the bus. Half-ass listening to the twenty-something preacher tell a joke, I fingered the envelope in my sleeve trying to guess what it was. Every time I started to pull it out, Bernard's face flashed before my eyes stopping me. Interrupting my thoughts, the preacher raised his voice and shouted, "God says to forgive those who do you wrong, brother and sisters. He says this so you'll understand His forgiveness. There is nothing you can do to deserve it. But when you forgive your enemy..."

Squirming to get comfortable in the pew, I took a deep breath, "Ivan must have—"

The preacher rapped the pulpit with his knuckles and lowered his voice, "God brings people into your life for a reason."

Nodding, I mumbled, "Stefon used to say that all the time."

"You may not understand why..."

I raised an eyebrow. "He used to say that too."

"Look at Job...God allowed the Devil to take everything away from Job...his wealth, his home, even his family..."

"Yeah, I sympathize with the guy. It seems, He let everything around me crumble, too." Pulling the envelope from my sleeve, I slid my finger under the flap and opened it to the sound of the preacher slapping his hand on the hard wooden surface of the pulpit. He then yelled, "BUT!...Job didn't complain." Stepping away from his notes, the preacher pointed at me, "And the Lord gave Job back double what he had lost."

Several bodies shot up out of their chairs waving their arms, followed by many loud amens. Nodding my head, I took a deep breath and sighed. "Well, Stefon. That would be a start towards convincing me."

"My friends..." spreading his arms wide, the preacher continued, "He is outside the door waiting for you. To fill your needs..." pausing, he bowed his head.

Reaching inside the envelope, I whispered to myself, "I wish Stefon was here to listen to this guy." While the preacher remained silent I pulled from the manila envelope an American passport with a driver's license stapled to it. Both bore the name Kezel Romanoff. Next came an Honorable Discharge certificate, bearing Kezel's name too. Clipped to the top of the last piece of paper, was a house key. Looking at the unfamiliar court document, I read the first line;

'To All Those Concerned, Be It Known, That Kezel Romanoff Has Been Adopted By Richard Bernard...and shall inherit.........'

CHAPTER TWENTY-ONE

The next morning, taking a cab from the motel where I spent the night, to the address on the paper. I looked at the characterless stucco building with matching numbers to the scrap piece of paper in my hand before opening the cab door. "Are you sure this the place?"

The driver glanced at me in his mirror. "It's the address you gave me."

"Do you know what it is?"

"Not a clue. Now if you don't mind, I have another fare to pick up."

I slammed his door shut. "Sheesh, why is it I get a strange feeling every time I step from a cab, that somethin's not right?" Walking over to the glass door, I looked through it at the interior design of the office.

The lady at the front desk, seeing me, pushed a button on her desk and motioned for me to come in. Cautiously stepping inside, the NorthStar logo on the far wall jumped out at me. "Uhmm, I think I'm in the wrong place."

"Come in, come in." The receptionist stepped around to the front of her desk with her hand out. "We've been expecting you, Mister Romanoff."

"Wait a min..." I pulled my hand back. "How do you know who I am?"

"Please, if you'll just follow me, everything will be explained."

"Uhh, no. The last time someone said that to me, I got shot at and went for a wild ride into the desert."

"We found the bus. You don't have to worry about Ms. Himmel anymore. Now if you don't mind, Mister Romanoff..." she pointed into a hallway, "please follow me.

Following her into the corridor, she stopped at the open door of a small conference room. "Please take a seat...Mister Hansen will be with you shortly. May I get you a cup of coffee?"

"Is he the lawyer that tracked me down 'cause of that damn parking ticket?" I asked, slipping past her into the mahogany paneled room. Dropping into one of the padded leather and chrome chairs, I squirmed back into it. "Tea, please."

She smiled, "Sugar?"

"No."

"Cream?"

"You ask a lot of fff... .Sorry, no. Just plain tea."

Still smiling, she nodded, "Yes sir."

'Don't call me... oh what the hell." Seeing the ashtray in the center of the table, I pulled the last one out the pack of Russian cigarettes Pavel had given me. Lighting it, I tossed the empty package on the table. "Ahh, I'm gunna miss those people."

"What makes you think that?" A voice from behind me asked.

Setting Tomas' lighter on the table so that the message inscribed on it was visible, I leaned back in the chair. "Cause, they're either dead, still in Siberia, or somewhere in between." Glancing at the fifty-ish man standing in the doorway, I placed the cigarette in the ashtray. "And who may you be?"

"Good morning Mister Romanoff, my name is Hansen. I'm the head attorney for NorthStar." Tossing the file in his hand on the table, he sat down across the table from me. "And I guarantee, you as a member of the Board, you'll be hearing from your friends quite often."

"What do you mean," I squinted at him, "member of the board?"

"My apologies..." he scooted his chair in and flipped open the file. "I just heard that Mister Bernard did not have time to fill you in."

"I barely had time to meet the man."

"So I understand." He slid the top page from the file in front of me. "As his only heir, you now own a controlling portion of NorthStar, and a chair on the Board. Please sign here at the bottom...saying you accept the seat."

"Uhh..." I patted my shirt pocket. "I don't have a pen. And who says I want—"

"Now..." pulling one from the breast pocket of his jacket, he laid it on the next form in the file and slid it towards me. "This is the deed to your house just outside Scottsdale. Sign there, next to the X."

"I don't have a house."

"You do now. Sign it, please. And..." Hansen glanced at another form, "this one is...a... non-disclosure for—"

"For what? How I got kidnapped. And was used to swindle the East Ger—"

"No." He slid the paper in front of me. "It's saying you'll not disclose the names of those who brought you home. Nor, how you got home."

"No." Shoving it back at him, I grinned, "Why shouldn't I tell the world?"

"Because, your friends now work for us." He gently pushed the form in my direction.

"Mister Romanoff, we're a defense contractor—"

"Whoopi. You make things for Uncle Sam."

Hansen gave me an exasperated look. "You don't know? Do you?"

"Phft," I shook my head.

"We gather data and make things happen for the Pentagon."

Staring at him for a moment, then glancing at the artwork on my arm as I scratched it, a thought occurred to me. "Hot damn," I slapped the table, "the godfather nailed it. He said some day I'd be making money passing along information." Sitting back in my chair, I slid my finger around in a circle on the table while asking, "Speaking of that, am I compensated for being on the board?"

"Handsomely. Now—"

"Can I go back... you know... to see Stefon and Arek?"

"I doubt it." Hansen leaned back in his chair. "That topic wasn't on the agenda. But, why do you ask?"

Hansen watched me as I pick up the empty Russian cigarette package. "I owe those two a lot. I vowed that if I could, I would help Stefon build an orphanage. And Arek, a school where he could teach kids machine shop. You know..." scratching the corner of my mouth with my thumb, I held up the package and stared at it. "Stefon came to the conclusion that the only way to topple the Soviets, would be to teach the children the truth. Letting their distaste for communism multiply," I suddenly crushed the package, "and crumble from within."

I could see the light of grand ideas illuminate in Hansen's eyes.

"Now that you've put it that way, I think..." he glanced over at the door, "I think being as you speak the language and are familiar with their culture, it could be arraigned. You couldn't go as a tourist. We would have to generate some kind of cover for you...maybe, some kind of charity organization......

Also by Kezel Romanoff

BETRAYED
BETRAYED The Eyes of the Tiger

Standalone
The Tales of Thaddeus and Katerina
He Stopped Loving Her Today
Betrayed